LOVE AND MURDER AT THE MANOR

BY PENNY TOWNSEND

Copyright © 2025 by Author Penny Townsend

All rights reserved. No part of this book may be used or reproduced in any form whatsoever without written permission, except in the case of brief quotations in critical articles or reviews.

This book is a work of fiction. Names, characters, businesses, organizations, places, events, and incidents are either the product of the author's imagination or used fictitiously. Any resemblance to actual persons, living or dead, events, or locales is entirely coincidental.

About the Author

Penny Townsend lives in Hampshire. Love and Murder at The Manor; is her third title in the Faye Lantern Mysteries with a Hint of Romance, Series.

As a qualified Life Coach and Counsellor, she has a unique perspective on our human qualities, which shines through in the characters she creates.

Penny usually sits in her hanging chair surrounded by colorful cushions, sipping tea from her cat mug while trying to keep her lovable and clumsy dog from knocking the cup over with his tail.

But most often, you'll find her at her desk, writing the next in the series of the Faye Lantern Mysteries.

CONTENTS

- Chapter One Faye 6
- Chapter Two The Manor Ball 11
- Chapter Three Grace 22
- Chapter Four After the Party 27
- Chapter Five Gossip 33
- Chapter Six The Hospital 37
- Chapter Seven Joe 47
- Chapter Eight Colby 57
- Chapter Nine Murder... 62
- Chapter Ten The Crime Scene 65
- Chapter Eleven Mrs Field.. 68
- Chapter Twelve Elizabeth.. 78
- Chapter Thirteen Young and Spirited 83
- Chapter Fourteen Glenda... 90
- Chapter Fifteen Elizabeth 97
- Chapter Sixteen Grace 102
- Chapter Seventeen An Unexpected Liaison 113
- Chapter Eighteen Reg... 119
- Chapter Nineteen A Confession.................................. 128
- Chapter Twenty Mrs. Field.. 139
- Chapter Twenty-One Tommy 143
- Chapter Twenty-Two Reg.. 146

Chapter Twenty-Three A Promise 153

Chapter Twenty-Four Tom 161

Chapter Twenty-Five Colby 170

Chapter Twenty-Six The Letter 175

Chapter Twenty-Seven Evidence................................ 181

Chapter Twenty-Eight Good Fortune 187

Chapter Twenty-Nine Colin... 196

Chapter Thirty Red Tape 205

Chapter Thirty-One Edmund....................................... 210

Chapter One
Faye

Faye was walking back through the village when Gwen came rushing out of the bakery. The red hairband she wore pushed her blonde hair off her face, and she rushed forward to greet her. Faye moved the bag she was carrying from her left hand to her right side as Gwen threw her arms around her.

Not fooled by Faye's switching hands, Gwen let out an excited squeal as she stepped back. She had caught sight of a black dress inside the open bag, its sequins glinting as they caught the sun.

"Is that a new dress?"

Faye sighed. Just for once, she wished Gwen would not be so busy wanting to know everyone's business. A rush of heat came to her cheeks as Tom came to her mind, and she tried to shrug it off.

"It's just a dress from London."

Gwen's hand raised to either side of her cheeks as she gasped, "from London."

Faye's heart sank. She had made it sound far more glamorous than it was, and now Gwen would fire a million questions at her. She tried to play it down in a casual tone.

It's nothing special, but I realised I didn't have an evening dress, well, not one that would be elegant enough for an evening soiree at the Manor." This wasn't true, but knowing Tom would be there, she wanted something more exciting than the usual dresses she wore. Gwen was still looking at the bag and Faye shifted it back behind her body, shielding it from Gwen for fear of her opening it up and pulling the dress out in the street. Seeing Faye's white-knuckle grip on the handles of the bag, Gwen stepped back and clasped her hands together in delight.

"It's so exciting. I've only ever been to the Manor House once as a child, with my dad. He made a five-tier cake for Elizabeth's sister Colette for her 21st birthday."

Her mouth curved into a smile as she drifted away into the memory.

"I remember the grandeur of it all. The enormous chandelier sparkling down from the ceiling above the wooden stairs in the entrance hall. I remember the staircase had a red carpet with brass rails running right down the middle, until it reached the black and white chequered floor, and two huge Chinese, vases with flowers sat on tables on either side."

She did a little jump. "It's going to be so much fun tonight. I can't wait."

She angled her head slightly to the side with a glint in her eye.

"So, I'll see you there then." Her eyes cast quickly to the bag and back. "In your new dress." She beamed a smile,

"And Tom's going too." She let out a giggle and headed back into the bakery.

Faye comforted herself that even though nothing seemed to go unnoticed by Gwen, no one else had any idea how she felt about Tom, and she wanted to keep it that way. After giving up on the idea of a quiet life in the village, her mind drifted to the upcoming ball and the Percys. She couldn't turn down their invitation again. Elizabeth had asked her to attend the last three parties, and she had now run out of excuses. Relieved to have arrived back at the Station House, she put down the bag and took her coat off as Buster came bounding towards her, his tail flying around faster than a helicopter's blades. He went straight to the new bag to investigate its contents, sniffing and pushing his head into the opening.

She picked up the bag and laughed as she placed it on the hall table. "There's no food in there for you, Buster."

"Aunty Faye." Daniel burst into the hallway. "Come and see this." He beckoned her to follow him as he disappeared back into the sitting room. Daniel was standing, peering into a cardboard box as she walked in.

"What on earth?" She bent down and picked up a tiny white and ginger bundle of fur.

"I know, right? But I couldn't just leave them in the bin."

"The bin?" she repeated. Her heart melted as she held the kitten's tiny body. It was so small and vulnerable.

Buster came up and started licking the kitten's ears as it wriggled in her hand. Daniel reached in and picked up another black and white one.

"There's three of them all together."

She turned the kitten over in her hand. "They don't look more than a few weeks old. And you found them in the bin?"

Daniel put the kitten back in the box. "Yes. When I lifted the lid of the bin at the back of the office to put some old files in, I found the three of them huddled together in the rubbish."

Faye sighed. "How could someone do such a thing? And on such a cold night." The kitten meowed as she placed it carefully back in the box.

"I think they're hungry."

Daniel carried over a bowl and sat down on the floor. "I got this baby formula from the chemist." He picked up the ginger kitten and dripped some of the formula from a teaspoon onto its mouth. "I've called the vet. They said they could take them after they close tonight. So, I'll drop them off on my way to the Manor House."

Distracted by the kittens, Faye had forgotten momentarily about the ball.

Putting the kitten back and picking up another one, Daniel continued with the feeding, trying unsuccessfully not to spill milk everywhere as the kitten twisted in his hand.

"I hope it's not going to be a stuffy affair tonight."

The same thought had crossed her mind. "We'll just have to grin and bear it. Anyway, didn't you say the Percys are clients of yours now?"

Daniel's brows dipped forward as he frowned. "Yes. I suppose I'd better be on my best behaviour."

She laughed. "It's only for a few hours. And you could leave early. That's what I'm intending to do."

Daniel looked up at her. "Is inspector Rawlings coming tonight?"

Her words choked in her throat as she blushed. "Yes. I think so."

A smile curved one side of Daniel's mouth as he nodded and returned to feeding the kitten.

"Right. Well then. I better feed Buster his dinner. Come on, Buster." She tapped her leg with her hand, and Buster trotted behind her. Glad to be out of the conversation with Daniel. After feeding Buster, she headed upstairs with the party at the Manor in just a few hours, occupying her mind.

Chapter Two
The Manor Ball

Faye considered walking to the Manor House. However, the lanes would be dark, and she couldn't walk in heels along the dirt track that cut through the churchyard—not that she wanted to walk through the churchyard at night. A shiver ran down her spine at the thought. The telephone ringing interrupted her thoughts.

"Hello, Miss Lantern."

Faye recognised Inspector Rawlings's voice immediately.

"I was wondering if you were going to the Manor House this evening for the dinner party?"

Butterflies flitted in her stomach as she said,

"Yes. As a matter of fact,…." She had an uneasy feeling come over her. Why would he be calling her? Unless there was something wrong. She finished, "I am."

"It's nothing serious." He said, sensing her tone. "I was just wondering if you needed a lift."

"Oh. Well." Her mind churned over all the possibilities. Daniel was going to arrive late as he was stopping off at the vet. Then, the walk through the graveyard flashed in her mind.

"Yes. I would like that very much, Inspector."

She heard him clear his throat. "Good. Right. I'll pick you up at seven forty-five sharp."

"Thank you, Inspector. I'll be ready." She replaced the receiver with a sense of relief. Smiling to herself, then a thought suddenly occurred to her. Did she just agree to a date with the Inspector by accepting the lift?

Faye felt self-conscious as she stared back at her reflection in the mirror. Her black dress sparkled as she turned to the side and back again. Although the folds of the dress fell gracefully to the floor, it hugged her body, framing every contour. She chided herself. Why hadn't she just brought the plain dress? The doorbell rang, and an inner panic gripped her as she glanced at the clock. There was no time to change now. With one hand grabbing her high heels off the floor, she rushed down the stairs.

She peered around the sitting room door. The box of kittens was gone. Daniel must have left already. Her stomach churned as she caught a quick glance of herself in the hall mirror. It had been a long time since she had put her hair up, and seeing it swept up, she could see her mother's face staring back at her. Her long earrings sparkled, matching the petite diamond necklace that swooped gracefully across her neck, a gift from her grandmother before she passed away.

Her hand was shaking as she opened the door. Inspector Rawlings was standing there in a black dinner suit, white shirt, and bow tie. His blond hair was combed neatly back, if still a little unruly. Her mind flashed back to the day he held her close to him and the warmth of his body as he carried her from the rocks at the lighthouse. She looked away, self-conscious but also wishing she had the courage to tell him how she felt.

He was still staring at her, his mouth open as she looked back.

"Good evening, Inspector."

She clasped her hands awkwardly, not sure if this was an actual date or if she was reading too much into it.

He seemed to snap out of his thoughts and said, "Yes. Of course. Good evening, Miss Lantern."

Shutting the door behind her, Faye was relieved to see the inspector's own black Ford Anglia and not the police car parked on the road outside. As she walked along the path, her dress made a soft rustling sound, reminding her of how wonderful it felt to be dressed up and going out. Inspector Rawlings held the car door open for her, and she smiled, appreciating the gesture, feeling a warmth towards him that felt new and exciting. With butterflies in her stomach, Tommy, her lifelong love came to her mind. Seven years had passed since he had been declared missing in action, and she had let go of the thought of him coming back if she wanted to move forward with her life. Now she had met another Tom, and it felt strange to say he made her feel the same way.

She looked over at him as they drove through the village.

"Do you think it will be a stuffy affair tonight?"

He glanced across at her.

"In my experience, it's always a stuffy affair at these big houses. However, I'm usually in a working capacity. But you can guarantee it will be formal."

She nodded silently, the engine noise feeling oddly comforting as they drove over the cobbled stone road. A movement caught her eye as she stared out the car window.

"It looks like it's snowing."

The inspector craned his neck, peering through the windscreen above the steering wheel.

"It's coming down pretty quick. We could easily become stranded if this keeps up."

Grateful she wasn't walking, she glanced at his face, which lit up as they went under some street lights.

"Elizabeth and Edward have plenty of rooms for guests if the snow doesn't let up."

He didn't reply as he peered through the windscreen and slowed the car down.

"I thought I saw someone up ahead?"

The car headlights shone down the road, lighting the falling snowdrops as they fell to the floor. Faye followed the beams of light to the end of the dirt track. Her eyes straining to see in the darkness.

"I can't see anyone."

Inspector Rawlings slowed the car to a crawl, scanning the road ahead. Faye leant forward, peering through the windscreen.

"Oh, look. Over there, Inspector." She could just see the indents of footprints left in the snow. He stopped the car and got out. After looking about for a minute, he got back in.

"Whoever it was, they're gone now."

He turned out of the lane, and she noticed how beautiful the trees looked with a white dusting of snow, which showed no signs of letting up as large drifts blew across the road. Faye's jaw dropped, as they drove through the enormous iron gates, open for the party guests, inviting them up to the Manor House. Rows of windows across the front of the house were lit up, their orange glow falling softly outside onto the glistening snow, creating an almost magical feel. The gravel crunching under the car wheels only added to the grandeur as they pulled up. Turning the engine off, the inspector turned to her, his voice hesitant.

"Would you mind calling me Tom tonight rather than Inspector, as we are at a social gathering?"

His eyes connected with hers, and butterflies danced in her stomach again.

"Yes. You're right. It is a social occasion; I think it's about time we used our first names. Please call me Faye."

Relief washed over him, and a huge smile lit his face. She didn't see him smile very often, but she had never really spoken to him outside of his work before.

Careful to hold on to the door handle, Faye swung her feet out onto the snow-covered ground. The gravel made her unsteady in her heels. Tom rushed round the car and held out his arm. Thankful and quietly relieved, she walked up the stairs and into the Manor House with him. Two waiters rushed forward to take their coats as she took in the magnificence of the entrance hall. It was just as Gwen had described, with an enormous glittering chandelier hanging from the top of the ceiling and the red carpet running down the middle of the stairs to meet the chequered black-and-white floor where they now stood.

Elizabeth came rushing up to them. Her scarlet red lipstick was always the first thing Faye noticed about her. It highlighted her blue eyes, making them stand out. She was elegantly dressed in a long, pale blue satin dress with a swooping open back. It was the type of dress you could only pull off if you had the perfect frame, which Elizabeth did.

"Faye darling. You look positively radiant." She kissed Faye on either side of her cheeks.

"And how dashing you look, Inspector. What a perfect couple you make." Faye's heart jumped as Tom glanced at her.

"Do help yourselves to the buffet."

She waved her arm in the air to get the attention of an elderly lady just arriving, "Florence darling," and rushed off.

An awkwardness after Elizabeth left made her turn away from Tom and look across the room. A younger woman in a dazzling red dress wore a diamond bracelet that caught the light as she took a cocktail glass from the silver tray the waiter held in his white-gloved hands. A large, well-rounded man was smoking. His plump fingers holding an equally plump cigar, his hands gesturing as he spoke. Her throat constricted, and she felt a sudden need to breathe fresh air, to be free from the swelling crowd of people and the noise of the band that had just struck up.

Tom was talking to an elderly man who was proudly sporting a row of medals pinned across the front of his navy blazer. She touched Tom's arm and whispered,

"I need some fresh air. I'm going outside for a minute." And quickly made her way to the side of the hall, avoiding the entrance that was overflowing as more people arrived. An arched wooden door, ornately carved with acorns and leaves, caught her eye. She turned the handle, thankful as it opened. A long corridor stretched out before her. The walls were lined with portraits of men in military uniform astride horses and beautiful women in regal clothes adorned in jewels sitting upright and serene in velvet chairs. Their eyes seemed to follow her as she walked along. A door to the left was ajar. She stepped inside a small but exquisitely decorated room scattered with floral sofas and chairs. A small writing bureau sat in the corner.

Elizabeth was scribbling a note and looked up, startled to see her. "Darling"

Faye's cheeks flushed. "Elizabeth. My apologies. I didn't know anyone was in here." She glanced around the room. "I was looking for a door to go outside and catch my breath. I'm afraid it was all getting a bit too much for me. Please excuse me." She went to leave, but Elizabeth's smile reassured her.

"Oh, darling, we all have to escape at times."

Filled with relief, she relaxed. Elizabeth walked out from behind the bureau toward the floor-length green velvet curtains and swept them back to reveal two enormous glass panelled doors.

"There's a balcony here if you want to take a minute to yourself."

Edmund appeared in the doorway looking hot and bothered, sweat running down his forehead.

"There you are, Elizabeth. And Faye." His eyebrows raised as his eyes swept up and down her, a smile creasing his mouth. "You are looking rather beautiful, if I may say so."

Her cheeks burned with heat. She wanted the ground to open and swallow her up as she thanked him and turned to the balcony doors.

Elizabeth grabbed his arm and ushered him out. "Faye needs some peace without you drooling over her, darling. Come, we can't both be missing from our own party."

The room fell silent as Faye turned the key and pulled the doors back. An icy blast of air took her breath away. She braced herself against the night air as she stepped out, wrapping her arms around her body, trying to keep warm. If only she had remembered her coat. At least it felt magical to see snowflakes falling down. She could hear the music from the other room softly playing, and her eyes drifted to the shadows being cast from the moonlight along the trees that edged the woods. Was that a voice she heard? She peered out across the grounds, just able to make out a shadowy figure disappearing into the darkness.

"Faye."

Hearing her name, she turned. Tom was standing there, holding her coat in his outstretched hands.

"I thought you might need this."

His voice soft and mesmerising; her heart leapt at the sight of him. She hadn't realised how much she was shivering and was grateful to feel the coat's warmth on her back as Tom wrapped it around her shoulders. She turned to face him. His blue eyes, staring into hers, made her feel weak, vulnerable and alive all at the same time. He moved closer. The longing in his eyes made her breathless. His mouth brushed her lip, sending a quiver down her spine and she gave in to his kiss, gently putting her arms around his neck. Nothing else mattered as he held her close. Her heart raced as he pulled away and said,

"Faye, I'm..."

Gunshots firing out pierced the air, making her jump, stopping him mid-sentence.

"What in Hell's fire..."

They both turned to stare, peering into the darkened tree line of the woods that engulfed the Manor House grounds. There was no movement anywhere that either of them could see, and irritated, Tom sighed.

"I better take a look. Will you be alright here?"

She nodded.

His reluctant steps quickened as he walked back inside through the house and into a group of panicked guests.

Faye watched the beams of several torch lights shine in zig zag motions across the blanket of snow falling heavily on the ground as Tom and a few other men from the party rushed into the estate gardens. They stopped at the end of the open field, their torches searching up and down along the tree line before they grouped back together and ran into the woods, the beams of light fading with them as they disappeared, and the grounds fell into darkness again. She made her way back inside the dimly lit room and closed the balcony doors, locking them with the key. Tom's kiss lingering in her mind, she smiled, glowing with happiness. She turned around and let out a scream as a young woman stood in the doorway – splattered blood covered her long blonde hair and face. Her bloodied hand holding on to the doorframe as she stared blankly into space, she opened her mouth as if she was going to say something, then stumbled into the room. Stopping a few feet away, fear raced across her eyes as she stared at Faye, then collapsed into a heap on the floor.

Chapter Three
Grace

Elizabeth came rushing into the room, closely followed by an out-of-breath Lady Florence, who was bedecked in jewels, from the tiara on her head to her dangling teardrop earrings, diamond necklace, and sparkling bracelets. Her dress billowed out from her waist in a green bouffant-style ball gown. She let out a high-pitched scream as she saw the young woman lying on the floor.

Inspector Rawlings came rushing in behind Edmund. His jaw tensed as he saw the body of the woman lying on the floor, covered in blood. He looked over to Faye, the relief on his face clear, as he saw she was unharmed. He bent down next to the young woman and placed two fingers on her neck.

"She's alive."

Elizabeth let out an audible gasp of relief as the girl stirred. The last thing she needed was Florence paltering the story, letting everyone believe a murder had taken place at the House.

Edmund straightened up. "Jolly good. I'll fetch her a glass of water from the kitchen."

He left, leaving Elizabeth standing over her, a sour look crinkling her nose up.

"Well, she's not one of my guests, Inspector. Just look at the ways she's dressed."

Elizabeth's comment fell on deaf ears as the inspector noticed the young woman coming to and helped her sit up, resting her back against the wall. Edmund came rushing back in with the water, handing it to the inspector.

She was thin, Faye noticed, and her jeans were torn at the ankle. She glanced at her bloodstained hands as she moved.

Grace opened her eyes to see a group of people gathered around her and a man knelt down beside her.

"You're safe," he said as her eyes widened, falling on Elizabeth.

"Mom?"

There was a stunned silence, except for Florence, who gasped as everyone turned to look at Elizabeth. Elizabeth's expression as she stared in horror was quickly replaced with her usual smoothing of things over. She glanced at the blood in the young woman's hair.

"Darling, you've had a nasty bump to your head. I'm not your mother." Her poise was now serene again as she raised her nose slightly.

Grace's hand fumbled in her pocket.

"Steady now," the inspector cautioned her.

She stared at him and pulled out a photograph from her pocket, holding it out to Elizabeth.

"See."

Elizabeth's eyes widened, her mouth falling open, as the inspector reached out and took the photograph. His eyes dropped to the blood-stained fingerprint clinging to one corner, before he looked at the photograph of a young Elizabeth holding a baby wrapped in an embroidered shawl.

"You're my mom, Elizabeth. I'm Grace. Aunt Collette named me after you. It's your middle name."

Elizabeth took one look at the photograph and staggered back, the colour draining from her face before she fainted, Edmund only just catching her before she hit the floor. After a tense few minutes, Edmund managed to revive Elizabeth with some smelling salts waved under her nose, which Lady Florence happened to have in her silk purse, as she had once fainted several years ago and felt compelled to carry them with her everywhere she went after that. Tom rang for one of his men to take Grace to the hospital and, satisfied all was in order, left with Faye. She looked over at Tom in the driving seat. "Well, that was a fine to do." Her mind recalled the sight of a blood-soaked Grace appearing in the doorway in front of her. "Quite shocking, actually...What do you think will happen to her?"

Tom was concentrating on navigating the snow-covered roads and drove cautiously out the Manor House gates.

"I need to determine whose blood is on her clothes and why it is there, before I can answer that."

She wouldn't say what had happened to her, which made his job all the more difficult.

"I'll know more once I get her clothes sent to the lab for testing." He wiped the inside of the windscreen with the jacket of his sleeve. "I'm going to the hospital tomorrow to interview her and see if I can make sense of all this."

Faye couldn't help feeling disappointed that Grace's appearance had overshadowed her perfect moment with Tom on the balcony.

"Poor Elizabeth. What a scandal it's going to be, having her daughter turn up out of the blue like that."

"Let's not jump to conclusions just yet, Miss Lantern."

Faye's stomach jumped at hearing Tom call her Miss Lantern. She turned to look at him, the surprise on her face unnoticed as he concentrated on steering, counteracting the car's wheels, locking and sliding across an icy patch of road.

"Of course, we still need to find out what that gunshot was all about."

She turned back, the sting of tears trickling down her face. Had their kiss meant so little to him? She wiped her cheek with the back of her hand, unseen in the darkness of the country lane. The rattle of the engine was now a different type of comfort, masking her shaky voice as she recomposed herself.

"Maybe it will come to light once you interview her tomorrow."

Faye continued the conversation until the Station House came into view. Turning the engine off, Tom ran around to open the car door for her.

"Well, thank you for the lift, Inspector. It certainly was an eventful evening. Good luck tomorrow with Grace."

As she stood by the car, the moonlight lit his face, and she could see a look of surprise and bewilderment as she walked away from him. Without looking backwards, she stepped into the Station House and closed the door behind her.

Chapter Four
After the Party

Faye heard Daniel whistling in the kitchen as she came down the stairs.

A beaming smile stretched across his face as she walked into the kitchen. "I hope you don't mind, Aunty Faye. I ran out of milk." He tipped cereal into his bowl, still whistling as he poured over the milk.

"Not at all." She glanced over at him. "You seem happy this morning."

His smile even broader now. "I've got a new client. An overseas investor and he's coming into the office today."

She smiled. It was good to see Daniel so happy. "That's good news."

Last night's ride home with Tom flashed in her mind, and her heart sank. She busied herself with finding a cup and saucer and poured out a tea from the pot Daniel had just made.

"I didn't see you at the Manor House last night."

"Oh, I timed it perfectly just as all hell broke loose." His smile disappeared as he poured out another tea. "I had to go with Inspector Rawlings and a few men from the party into the grounds after the gunshot happened. All in our dinner jackets, I half expected Al Capone to pop up from behind the bushes and lead the charge."

Faye's stomach felt like it had been gut-punched at the mention of Tom's name again.

"Did you find anything?" she asked casually, feeling Buster put his head on her hand.

"Not a sausage. And I can tell you I was mighty glad to get back. It's pretty creepy in the woods at night."

Daniel noticed Faye stroking Buster's head as Buster's tail wagged, hitting the side of his chair with a thud.

"We could have done with Buster there last night. His tracking skills would have quickened everything up."

He stuffed a spoonful of cornflakes into his mouth.

"It wasn't all bad, though," he mumbled, trying to speak and eat at the same time.

"I met my new client there. An American guy called Joe. He wants me to show him around the village before he leaves."

A knock on the door sent Buster rushing down the hallway.

"Inspector," Daniel announced as he opened the Station House Door. "Do come in. What do we owe the pleasure?"

Taking his hat off, the inspector bent down to pat Buster.

"Just a routine call about last night."

Daniel nodded as he led him down the hallway and into the kitchen.

Faye's heart leapt out of her chest as he walked in. His face strained as he looked at her.

"Miss Lantern."

She could hear the tension in his voice as she stared at him, her heart pounding.

"I've come to check on you after last night."

Her mind raced to the crestfallen look on his face as she left him standing by the car and walked away. Her cheeks flushed, and she turned towards the sink with her back to him.

"I'm fine, Inspector. You needn't worry about me. I'm sure you have other urgent police business to attend to."

Daniel stopped eating and looked at Faye and then at the inspector as the cup slipped from her hand and crashed into the sink.

The inspector walked over to her. "Let me help you."

"No. Thank you." Her cheeks reddened again as she picked up the broken pieces of china.

Daniel jumped up. "I have some paperwork to sort out upstairs, and I don't want to be late."

Faye spun around. "Oh. Really. Can't you stay for a bit?" She was desperate not to be left alone in what was rapidly becoming an awkward situation. The look of surprise on Daniel's face made her realise she was making things worse. He winked at her.

"I'll leave you two to have a lovely chat." He smiled and nodded at the inspector as he left.

Oh, Gods. This was awkward. She wished she was anywhere but alone with Tom, in stark contrast to the pure joy she felt in his arms last night as he kissed her.

She walked to the far end of the kitchen and dropped the broken pieces in the bin, waiting for him to speak. There was silence, and after a few moments, she turned around to look at him.

"There you are," he said, holding her gaze as he walked over.

Anger rising in her, she snapped. "What do you mean?" Knowing he was waiting for her to engage with him fully and make eye contact.

"I mean," he said, moving closer to her. "I want to ask you what happened last night. You changed suddenly on the way home and became distant."

He placed his hat on the kitchen counter, and her body trembled at his closeness. She looked down, a mixture of guilt and anger swirling inside her head.

Lifting her chin up with his hand. His touch making her catch her breath.

"Faye."

She was still angry as she pulled her head away from him.

"Really, Inspector. I don't think calling me Faye is appropriate right now."

He recoiled like a wounded animal. "But I thought we had come to an understanding last night."

She pursed her lips, defiance bubbling up as she stared at him.

"Is that just when you want to kiss me? Because I distinctly remember you calling me Miss Lantern in the car on the way home. So, I believe that was the end of our social understanding."

She folded her arms and glared at him as he searched for words. He realised there had been a moment in the car, and he was so used to calling her Miss Lantern he had forgotten when they were talking about the evening's events.

His brow furrowed into lines as he stared back at her. "Is that what's bothering you? Faye, I was thinking about work. It was unintentional."

She threw her hands up defiantly and went to walk away, but he stepped forward. He was so close to her that she froze, her heart pounding. She could easily have ducked around him, but she didn't.

"Faye. I meant what I said. I want to be on first-name terms." He leaned forward, his lips almost touching hers. "Tell me to leave now, and I won't bother you again."

His eyes fixed on hers, her breath caught. Now, more than ever, she wanted the soft touch of his lips upon hers. His eyes softened as she fell silent. The warmth of his hand brushed her cheek, and her heartbeat quickened as his arms gently fell around her, pulling her into his kiss.

Chapter Five
Gossip

Faye hummed to herself as the morning went on. Buster went and fetched his lead from the hall table and brought it back to her. He sat with it dangling out of his mouth, his tail thumping wildly on the floor behind him. She smiled.

"Come on, then. I have to go to the village, anyway." And grabbed her coat from the hallway.

The air was crisp as she stepped outside. The sun was shining, and she felt alive for the first time in months, but guilt nagged at her as she walked along. What if Tommy was still alive? She said she would wait for him. They had been together since their teenage years, but after waiting so long already,…her heart sank at the realization she had to accept he wasn't coming back after all this time. A gentle breeze lifted her hair as she walked into the village, Buster trotting happily beside her.

Hector Alewood, the village butcher, waved through the shop window at her. Buster leant on the lead, dragging her forward, his tail wagging furiously as they went inside. Faye never liked the smell of sawdust mixed in the air and turned her head away to cough.

"I have your order ready, Faye. And a nice juicy bone for Buster."

"Oh, you really shouldn't spoil him, Hector."

He shook his head. "It's my treat."

He was an enormous man, and his blue and white striped apron didn't quite meet at the back of his large frame. He wrapped the pork chops in paper and passed them to her. She noticed he always seemed to have red hands as he bent down to give Buster his bone. Buster took his offering and sat on the floor, sniffing it over, deciding which was the best place to start.

"Faye." Gwen's voice called out as she hurried into the butcher's shop.

"Morning Hector." She handed him a sticky bun in a box and his eyes lit up. His large hands covered the box as he took it from her.

"I'm going to have this with a cup of tea." And excused himself to put the kettle on.

Gwen had wrapped her blonde hair up in a blue and white scarf, tied into a bow on the top that flopped about as she moved her head.

"What a carry-on that was last night."

Faye's mind immediately jumped to Tom, and a feeling of happiness washed over her.

"Yes. It was all a bit alarming. I didn't see you there."

"Oh. I was in the ballroom dancing with a rather handsome duke." Her mouth pulled back into a smile as she sighed.

"That was until the gunshot went off, and then we found out Elizabeth," she gasped. "Of all people, has a secret child."

"Well, let's not jump to conclusions, Gwen." She realised she was repeating Tom's words from last night.

Gwen sighed again, this time in frustration.

"But the woman had a photograph of Elizabeth holding her as a baby."

"It's not been proven yet. Elizabeth hasn't said anything about who the baby was she was holding."

Gwen threw her hands up in the air, dismissing Faye's idea of Elizabeth's innocence.

"All I know is you don't go fainting if you haven't got anything to hide."

Faye secretly felt the same way but didn't answer her. Gwen tilted her head slightly.

"By the way, where were you last night? I looked for you in the hall and the ballroom. I couldn't find you anywhere.?"

She stared at her, waiting for an answer.

"I needed some fresh air."

Gwen jumped in excitedly before she could finish.

"You went outside. Did you see who shot the gun?"

"No. No. I was on the balcony." Her face blushed red as Gwen's eyes bore into her.

"Were you with someone?"

"No. I just went on my own. I needed to get away from all the people for a bit."

Uncomfortable at telling Gwen a lie, she looked away." Why couldn't she just mind her own business?"

Gwen was still studying her face as Hector reappeared behind the counter, and she saw her chance to escape.

"Thank you for Buster's bone, Hector. Come on, Buster." She pulled at his lead.

"Bye, Gwen."

She rushed out the door, leaving Gwen with a puzzled look on her face.

Chapter Six
The Hospital

It had been two days since Faye had seen Tom. Frustrated at not hearing from him, her mind was working overtime, coming up with reasons for his absence. He was obviously busy with the young woman's case, but it didn't make her feel any better.

The telephone ringing made her jump.

"Gwen. What a surprise." She prayed she wouldn't have to lie to her again if she asked more questions.

"I've got a message from Tom."

Faye's heart missed a beat.

"Tom?"

"Yes. He wants you to go down to the police station and give a statement, as a witness, about the young girl."

"Oh. Yes. Of course." Her mind searched for reasons why Tom had asked Gwen, to pass the message on to her, instead of speaking to her himself.

Noting the silence, Gwen started,

"I took him in some lunch, and he was rushed off his feet with work and short staffed. He asked me to apologise to you for not calling you sooner."

A pang of jealousy curdled Faye's stomach. "I see."

"So ..." Gwen said, drawing out her words. "You two have a thing going on."

Faye nearly dropped the receiver. She placed her other hand on it to steady herself.

"I don't know what you mean?"

Gwen was silent for a moment. "My brother never uses first names unless he's close to someone. And he used your name when he asked me to call you."

"Your brother?" Faye was flabbergasted that in all the time she had been in Petworth - for over a year, Gwen had never told her that Tom was family to her.

"Now we have got that cleared up; maybe you and Tom could stop by for dinner next week?"

Faye let out a sigh. She knew Gwen wouldn't let her off the hook. It would be foolish to try to convince her otherwise.

"I'll let you know." She said and rushed off the telephone. Now Gwen knew there was a possibility she may let it slip, and she would have to put up with the knowing looks of the villagers, who were always in each other's business far too much for her liking.

She walked down to the station with mixed emotions. On the one hand, she was glad to see Tom but also annoyed he hadn't called her himself. Gwen inviting them to dinner as a couple was also on her mind, as though she was in a full-blown relationship with him.

Tom looked surprised as she walked in. Files were piled up on his desk, and his face was drawn and tired, like he hadn't slept for days. A broad smile swept across his mouth.

"Faye." He went to step forward to her and stopped. His eyes full of longing, changing to a stern gaze as Pemberley walked in with another file.

"I need you to do a witness statement for the evening of the Manor House Ball. It's police procedure. Official procedure," he added.

She could tell by his authoritative tone and the distance he held between them he was trying to make sure she understood he would act as an inspector whilst she was there for the witness statement. And would probably call her Miss Lantern.

The corners of her mouth tugged into a smile. "It's alright, Inspector. I understand."

She could see him struggling with his emotions, the longing in his eyes to be close to her. Her heart felt the same desire, and only Pemberley, still in the room, kept them apart.

As she gave her statement, she recalled the blood covering the young woman.

"Have you found out who the blood on her belonged to, Inspector?"

He sat down wearily as Pemberley was scribbling down Faye's statement.

"It's not her blood. The lab has confirmed that much." He rubbed his hands over his face in frustration. "But she won't say whose it is."

"Perhaps I could speak with her? After all, I was the first person she saw, and maybe she would open up more to me."

He didn't reply, and she could see he was thinking it over.

"Well. If that's all, Inspector." She stood up as he said,

"I think it's worth a try, Miss Lantern. Are you able to go to the hospital with me now?"

Hope lingered in his eyes as he stared at her.

Relishing the time to be with him, she smiled.

"Of course."

He turned to Pemberley, who was already standing.

"Can you tell the desk sergeant to hold all my calls? You know where I'll be if you need me."

Pemberley nodded. "Right, you are, sir." And disappeared, Faye's statement clutched in his hands.

She followed Tom outside to the waiting police car. She wasn't expecting him to open the car door for her and quickly got in.

"Is it far, the hospital from here?"

He threw his coat onto the back seat as he sat down. She felt a twinge of excitement rush up her spine as he looked at her.

"Ten minutes or so, not far at all."

She nodded. "Did you find out if Grace was her real name?"

He tensed his jaw. "Not officially. We only have her word on that."

Faye looked out the window at the thatched cottages fading behind them as they headed out of the village.

"Is that snow again?" She said as flakes drifted down, hitting the windscreen.

"I think we are in for a worse bout of it than the other night." He glanced over at her and back again. A smile formed across his face.

Was he thinking about their first kiss on the balcony? Her stomach turned with a million butterflies. So much had happened between them in the last couple of days.

"It was a strange evening, full of surprises, good and bad."

He turned to her again, a playful glint in his eye. "I like to think the good outweighed the bad."

She could feel her cheeks flush as she smiled. A glow of happiness welling up inside her. They turned the corner to see the hospital building looming in the distance. An ambulance raced past them, its sirens blaring as they pulled up.

The hospital was a hive of activity as nurses rushed about on high alert, preparing for casualties from an accident at a local factory. She waited as Tom spoke to a nurse and looked around for a seat. She gasped, stepping back to narrowly avoid a trolley that came dashing past with a teenage boy lying unconscious on it. A doctor with a pained expression ran next to the trolley, accompanied by another nurse, as they sped along the corridor.

She could see there was a problem as she watched Tom having an intense conversation with a nurse who pointed to the clipboard in her hand and shook her head. Tom's furrowed brow and quick pace as he walked back confirmed her fears as he reached her.

"Grace has gone."

Faye was trying to process his words as he said,

"They don't know how it happened. But probably, in all the confusion going on with the accident, she slipped past them."

He shook his head. "They have no record of her leaving. She must have just walked out."

He shrugged. Annoyance clinging to his face.

Faye shared his disappointment. She was hoping she could help her.

"Had you arrested her?"

"No. It's not a crime to have someone else's blood on you. Not unless they suddenly turn up dead."

He glanced at her. "I'm sorry you had a wasted trip."

She stood up. "I'm happy to be here. I just wish I could have been more help to you."

As more people were being rushed in on trolleys, his face turned to concern.

"We'd better head back. The telephone will be ringing off the hook at the Station by now."

Happy to leave, she quickened her pace to keep up with his stride as they left the hospital. She wondered if Grace had done something awful to end up being covered in someone else's blood. Maybe even murdered someone, and now she had fled.

As the hospital faded out of view, they drove back towards the village.

"Is there still a case now?"

He frowned. "It will be put on hold for a few weeks, and she will be noted as a person of interest to us on file. That's all we can do at this stage." He paused. "Unless anything else happens. And in my experience, it usually does."

She watched the white ducks bobbing up and down on the pond as they drove into the village.

"Oh, look. There's Daniel." He was standing outside the accountant's office he worked in, on the opposite side of the road, talking to a younger man in his early twenties by her reckoning.

Her eyes caught sight of the cowboy boots he was wearing.

"That must be Joe, the American investor Daniel is so excited about. He's a new client of his." Tom nodded, his mind elsewhere. As they pulled up outside the police station, she turned to face him as he said,

"I believe it's still my move in our chess game."

Her heart raced as his eyes held hers. She wanted to see him but didn't want to go out in front of the wagging tongues of the villagers. Not just yet anyway.

"Perhaps we could catch up on the game this evening?"

His face softened with relief as he took her hand.

"How about seven thirty?"

She wanted to kiss him right there in the police car but smiled instead,

"I look forward to it."

"Great. I'll see you tonight."

She got out and closed the car door behind her, wondering what she could wear that night as he drove away.

It was a fifteen-minute walk back to the station House, which didn't bother her at all. Everything looked brighter as she strolled through the village. Birds singing in the trees sounded more tuneful. The cobbled stone path had a soft layer of snow which crunched pleasantly underfoot. The rays of fading light were enough to make it glisten now and then. Turning in the lane, she hummed to herself as she reached the Station House and opened the front door. Hanging her coat up, she called out to Buster, waiting for him to come bounding down the hallway, tail wagging to greet her. She wondered if Daniel had taken him for a walk when he didn't appear. Her mind flashed to Daniel standing outside his office talking with his new client, and Buster wasn't with him.

"Buster!" she called out, opening the sitting-room door. She jumped as she saw Daniel, with a terrified look on his face, standing next to the American client he had been talking to in the village earlier.

"Daniel," she said, startled. His eyes were full of terror as she glanced at him and then across at Joe. He was wearing a red peaked cap and brown sheepskin jacket over blue jeans and brown leather cowboy boots. He had a southern drawl to his voice as he said,

"Close the door behind you."

He stared at her, his eyes dark and menacing, making her recoil in fear. Her hands trembled as she closed the sitting-room door, petrified to turn around and face him again.

Chapter Seven
Joe

"You have something I want."

She frantically searched her mind. "I'm not sure I understand?"

Her heart pounded as he stared at her, as if weighing her up.

"You have Grace. I want you to bring her here."

There was no misunderstanding of his intentions as she saw him push a small handgun into Daniel's shaking back. He was talking about Grace as though she was his possession rather than a person. His emotionless expression haunting. She would have to be careful with every word she said. Keeping her voice gentle but steady, she forced a half smile.

"I'm afraid I don't know where Grace is?"

His mouth pulled back into a sneer.

"I saw you get out of the police car with that copper at the hospital." Anger flashed across his eyes.

"Where is she?"

His voice, laced with bitterness hit her like a blast of cold air making her tremble.

"I'm so sorry, but Grace was already gone when we got there. The nurse told us she had already left, and they didn't see her go."

She could feel her breathing getting faster as she looked at him, praying he would leave once he realised she had no idea where Grace was.

"I'm not leaving until you bring Grace here. Get on the telephone and tell that cop to bring Grace here."

Faye didn't want Tom turning up later, walking into a deadly situation. If she could somehow make him realise there was something wrong, he would at least know what to do.

Her eye rested briefly on Daniel, his body trembling as she looked over. She nodded. "I'll call him now."

His deadly glare sent a chill down her spine.

"Don't get smart. I'll be listening to every word."

He shoved Daniel forward, pushing the gun into the small of his back, forcing him into the hall. She lifted the receiver and dialled the police station, her hand shaking as she clutched the telephone to her ear.

"Yes. Hello. I'd like to speak with Inspector Rawlings, please. It's Miss Lantern." She looked up briefly, feeling the icy stare of his eyes upon her. Her throat felt constricted as she said,

"Hello Inspector. It's Miss Lantern. I'm calling regarding the young woman, Grace. Her aunt has just shown up here, and I need you to bring Grace to the tea rooms immediately."

There was a pause at the end of the line.

"What, aunt? What are you talking about, Faye?"

"Yes, Inspector, I know you'll do your best."

Her stomach lurched as she saw Daniel stumble forward. The gun was now trained on them both as Joe's eyes, threatening, made her shudder in fear. She heard Tom say,

"Faye. What's going on?"

Desperate to make him understand, she made every word seem strange.

"I just feel Grace would want to be with her aunt. Thank you, Inspector. I'm glad you understand. Goodbye."

Still shaking, she quickly placed the receiver down and hoped he would be sufficiently confused to show caution at the least.

The telephone rang again making her jump. Good, that would be Tom ringing back, to find out what was going on.

Joe lowered his head and spat on the floor. He glowered at her in a slow, threatening manner as she went to pick up the receiver, and she backed away from the telephone.

He waved his gun, herding them back into the sitting room. He shoved Daniel forward.

"You. Sit on the floor."

Daniel dropped to the floor and sat with his back against the fireplace wall. Relief in his face at not having the gun pushed in his back any longer. Faye's eyes fell on the game of chess sitting on the table and her stomach churned at the thought of Tom, walking in, not knowing Joe was there with a loaded gun. She went to sit down in the chair when the doorbell rang out. She froze. Her heart racing. It couldn't be Tom. There wasn't enough time for him to get there that fast. Joe stood pointing the gun at Daniel.

I've got your nephew here. Just remember that and get rid of them. Faye took a breath in to compose herself as she opened the Station House door. Mrs Field was standing on the doorstep. Her thin, sharp features and thinning red hair were quite an odd look against her deep purple coat, which she had pulled up around her neck, braced against the snow which was falling heavily.

"Faye. Thank goodness. I need your help. I have a bit of a situation."

Faye stared blankly at her, pleading with her eyes to leave, which went completely unnoticed by Mrs Field as her gloved hands wrapped tightly around her body. She shivered, shifting from one foot to the other.

"Can I come in Faye?"

Faye lifted her head up and away from Mrs Field. Desperate for her to leave.

"I'm sorry. It's not a good time right now."

Mrs Field's eyes widened as her mouth dropped open. Faye always had time for people, and now she was busy? Undeterred, she raised her nose in the air.

"Well, perhaps you could come round to my cottage when you have a minute. I've helped a young girl I bumped into at the hospital." She shook her head. "But I'm not sure what to do. I think she needs help. She is in an awful state. I thought you could talk to her and find out what's got her so scared.

Faye could feel her heart sink in her chest. Grace was at Mrs Fields, and her mind was frantically searching for the right answer without alarming her.

"Give me ten minutes, Mrs Fields, and I'll come over."

Her face lit up.

"Oh. Well. Thank you. I knew I could rely on you, Faye. "

She felt a wave of panic run through her as she shut the front door and walked back down the hallway and into the sitting room.

A sickly smile had curved across Joe's mouth.

He raised the gun towards her. "We're leaving now."

He turned to Daniel.

"You! Get up."

Daniel shook as he stood up and followed Faye into the hallway.

He jumped as Joe shouted.

"Wait." And pointed to a cupboard under the stairs. His narrowed eyes glowering, fixed on him.

"In here."

Daniel ducked, barely missing a dustpan and brush hanging up, as Joe shoved him in and closed the door, locking it with the key.

Faye was glad Daniel would be left behind. He would be safe until Tom arrived to let him out and he could tell him where they were heading.

"Move. " He nudged her back with the gun.

Her heart racing, she started to walk to the front door.

"Not that way."

She felt his eyes boring into her as she turned around. He motioned with the gun.

"Through the back."

She made her way through the kitchen and out the back door. An icy blast of air made her catch her breath. Everything was covered in a white blanket of snow stretching across the tree lined lane, and over the fields opposite.

All the time they walked, her mind was on Mrs Field, who usually said what she thought in no uncertain terms and how she could keep her from saying anything to anger Joe and endangering all of them. She looked around. The lane was empty, apart from a horseback rider who trotted past them in a hurry, the horse's hooves thudding in the snow that was now getting deeper. Her feet were starting to go numb from the cold as they approached Mrs Field's cottage. A warm light filtered through a chink in the curtains, and the familiar smell of smoke from a log fire filled the air. Joe pushed her through the front gate and down the side path until they reached the rear of the cottage. He held the gun on her until her back was against the wall, and she stood motionless, only her warm breath visible, spiralling into white mist as she breathed out into the cold air. He peered in through the kitchen window, and she could see his hand grip tighter on the gun. Anger flashed in his eyes as he recoiled back and turned to her.

"Knock the door."

He slithered back against the wall in the darkness, just out of sight. Faye approached the back door. Her body trembling as she gently tapped on the door.

"Mrs Field. It's Faye."

Her eye caught the gun in Joe's hand rise up as she called out again.

The bolt on the back door clattered across and the door opened. A disgruntled Mrs Field stood there, staring accusingly at her.

"Faye! Why have you come through the back door? I left the front door open for you."

"Oh. I thought I would come through the lanes for a change. It's a lovely walk and I carried on down the path." She shrugged.

Mrs Field looked down at her wet shoes and back up again.

"Are you sure you are feeling okay, Faye?

Joe's raised hand with the gun pointed at her was in the back of her mind as she smiled,

"Yes. Perfectly fine, thank you. May I come in?"

A terrified scream rang through the air, rooting them both to the spot.

"What on earth?" Mrs Field stared at Faye momentarily, then ran back into the sitting room. Faye's heart was thumping out of her chest as she raced after her, nearly colliding into her as she stopped dead in the doorway. Joe was standing next to Grace, terror filled her eyes as she sobbed uncontrollably. His hand shaking in rage as he pulled her up from the chair. His grip tightened on her arm as Mrs field shouted,

"Release that young girl at once."

He fired a shot towards the ceiling, sending white pieces of plaster crashing to the floor, drowning out her voice.

"I'll say what's going to happen."

He pointed the gun towards them both as he backed out the door, his arm around Grace's neck, the gun in her back. He stopped and aimed the gun at Mrs Field's head as though deliberating. Every muscle in Faye's body tensed as fear immobilised her. Surely, he wasn't going to shoot them, not after letting Daniel go. It didn't make sense. She could hear the blood pulsing in her ears as his eyes narrowed. Grace's voice, shaking, cut through the silence, pleading.

"Don't hurt them, Joe. Please. You have me now."

Faye saw the muscles on his arm tense as he tightened his grip around her throat, stopping her from talking. Her arms dropped to her sides in silence as he spoke, still pointing the gun at Mrs Field, who stood trembling next to Faye.

"Follow me, or call the police, and I'll shoot you where you stand."

Mrs Field went to argue, but Faye gave her a hard nudge with her elbow, silencing her. Joe backed out the door and disappeared. She put her finger to her lips as Mrs Field went to speak again, listening as the latch on the back gate of the cottage clicked shut. He was leaving. She quietly headed to the window. In the fading light, she saw him pulling Grace down the lane by her arm, dragging her as she stumbled into the deepening snow.

Faye chose her words carefully, aware of Mrs Fields dislike of Tom; she didn't use his name.

"Mrs Field. Call the police station now."

She couldn't leave Grace in the hands of that monster and swung on her heel. There might still be a chance to catch them.

"Tell them Daniel is locked in a cupboard at the Station House."

Mrs Field stared wide-eyed as she rushed down the hall and out the kitchen door.

"Where are you going?"

Faye looked back and saw the fear in her eyes.

"Don't worry. I'll be fine. I'm going to follow them." Her legs felt the biting cold of the snow as she ran down the lane and out of sight.

Chapter Eight
Colby

Clouds of steam rose in the air from her breath as Faye watched the faint outline of three shadowy figures in the distance. Her eyes strained to see clearly through the falling snow. A scream rang out, sending a chill down her spine. Her stomach lurched in fear as what she thought looked like Grace's body fell to the floor. She wanted to run over, but her eye caught sight of the two men fighting, their arms flying as they grappled. Her whole body shook as she saw them crashing through the thicket. She stumbled forward, her legs like jelly, as she forced herself to run towards the body on the floor. As she drew close, her heart jumped into her mouth. With her long blonde hair flayed across the ground, Faye recognised Grace's limp body lying in the snow. She crouched down beside her. Thankful she couldn't see any blood, she placed her hand on Grace's face and gently moved her head to see a large swelling above her eye.

"Grace."

She stirred, opening her eyes. Terror filled them as she screamed and tried to sit up.

"Where's Colby?"

Faye put her hand on her shoulder. "It's okay, Grace. Relax."

Behind her, Faye heard the pounding of running footsteps in the snow, drawing closer. Her breathing grew faster. She turned to see Tom and Pemberley running towards her.

"Faye."

The sound of Tom's voice made her whole body crumble down in relief. He skidded in the snow as he reached her, kneeling down on one leg. She collapsed into him, burying her tear-stained face into his neck.

"I've got you." He whispered.

Still shaking, she pushed herself upright.

"Grace needs to get to the hospital. I think she has a concussion."

He glanced over at Grace, who was lying on the floor, her eyes drifting over to them.

"Pemberley, find Bennet and bring the car here."

"Right, you are, sir."

He rushed off towards the Station House, where they left Bennet on guard. Tom took off his coat and placed it over Grace.

His voice calm and reassuring her as he said, "Stay awake Grace. It won't be long, and my officer will have the car here to take you to the hospital."

He stood up, his hand reaching out to help Faye as she struggled to her feet.

Her eyes fell briefly on his clenched jaw as he looked at her.

"Mrs Field begrudgingly told me what happened. And, when I realised the danger you were in..."

His voice trailed off as he shook his head.

"The thought of losing you, I couldn't bear it."

Butterflies rose in her stomach as she held his gaze. Her heart beating fast as he pulled her in close to him.

In the pause between them, all she could hear was her breathing, his love kindling a flame in her heart she had long thought dead.

"Tom I…"

A crash in the bushes where the two men fighting had disappeared made them both turn. Tom instinctively took a step in front of Faye, shielding her with his body as a man in his twenties came stumbling out.

Faye felt an instant reflex to vomit as she saw his dark hair mixed with blood that trickled down his forehead. His hand was clamped to a wound on his arm, blood seeping through his fingers dripping onto his jacket. Tom raised his voice.

"Stop right there. Don't come any closer."

His eyes darted to where Grace was lying on the floor as Inspector Rawlings said,

"Who are you?"

Grace turned and screamed out, "Colby!"

He dashed to her side and dropped to the floor, throwing his arms around her. Tears ran down her face as she hugged him and then pulled back, terror gripping her eyes as she scanned the thicket behind him.

"What happened? Where's Joe?"

Colby's face was red and swollen. His lips bleeding, pain creasing his eyes as he spoke slowly.

"He ran off. Over that way." He pointed in the direction of the thicket at the same time looking at Tom.

Tom didn't take his eyes off of him, years of experience teaching him to watch for any change in the position of his body or sudden movement that would gain him a few valuable seconds and give him an edge if he became a threat.

"I can see you know Grace, but who are you?"

"I'm Colby. I came over to England with Grace."

Faye raised her hand in front of her eyes, blocking out the glare of the police car's headlights shining down the lane as it came into view, followed by a second police car. Pemberley threw the car door open and rushed out as he saw Colby standing there covered in blood.

Tom raised his hand.

"It's okay. Get this young lady to hospital and take Miss Lantern home." Bennette jumped out the second car and ran towards them.

"Bennette. Take this man into custody. Hold him in the car until I've worked out what's going on here…and wait for me before going to the hospital."

He turned and headed into the thicket, and Faye's stomach dropped. She hadn't had a chance to tell him how she felt, and now the moment had passed. She called out, making him turn.

"Tom. Be careful."

A brief smile crossed his mouth. He nodded and strode off, disappearing into the surrounding woodland as the cloak of darkness approached.

Penny Townsend
Chapter Nine
Murder

It was ten o'clock when Officer Bennette eventually dropped Faye back home at the Station House. She slumped wearily into the chair at the kitchen table. Daniel came rushing down the stairs behind Buster, who was the first to greet her. His wagging tail and frantic sniffing of her clothes, assessing where she had been like an interrogation, made her smile.

Daniel's face lit up, full of relief as he saw her.

"Aunty Faye. Thank the lord." He kissed her on both cheeks. "I've been out of my mind with worry."

He paused. "Are you okay?"

Although it was Tom's job to deal with these investigations, it still concerned her, and the image of him disappearing into the darkening woods lingered in her mind.

"I'm fine, Daniel. How about you? What happened after I left?"

He dragged a chair noisily out from under the table and sat down, placing his head in his hands. He shook his head, his eyes rolling up before sighing and putting his hands back down.

"It was a hideous nightmare being locked under the stairs. I would have preferred the bedroom. At least I could have had a lie-down."

Faye stifled a laugh as he continued,

"I was desperate when I heard him tell you to walk down the hallway, and when you left out the back door, I started shaking the cupboard door like a madman, hoping the key would fall out. Of course, I had put nothing down to catch it." He shrugged. "So, it just landed on the floor."

A smile stretched across her mouth, and unable to help herself, she stood up and reached over to hug him. Glad he was there, safe and well. It all could have turned out so much worse.

"I'm so relieved you are okay." She released him from her grip.

He nodded. A smile creeping across his mouth.

"My therapist will be delighted. At last I have real issues."

The doorbell rang, and Faye's heart lurched in fear as they looked at each other. A dread welled up in the pit of her stomach. Daniel stood up and glanced at the kitchen clock. It was midnight.

"Well, this can't be good." He said, walking off down the hallway.

Her breath caught in her throat as Daniel opened the door to see Tom standing there. A flicker of hesitation crossed his face as his eyes fell upon her. She knew instantly there was something wrong.

"Daniel, Faye, I need you both to come down to the station with me to make a statement…He paused. There's been a murder."

Love And Murder At The Manor

Chapter Ten
The Crime Scene

Tom's words jolted her stomach as she heard him say murder, and her mind instantly rushed to the snowy lane and Joe and Colby fighting.

"Is it Joe?"

Tom's mouth pulled back as he frowned. "Yes. And you were at the crime scene. Your evidence could be vital."

Daniel already had his coat on and was walking out the door with Buster on his lead. "I'm going to walk Buster down to the station. He glanced at Faye. I'll catch you up there."

He pulled his collar up around his neck as he stepped out. Faye picked up her coat. The last thing she wanted to do was go out again, but she knew it was important. As she found her gloves she could feel Tom staring at her. His face in the shadow as he stood in the doorway. She moved closer to him. She wasn't used to such deep emotion and took a breath in as she faced him.

"What you said when we were in the lane. I want you to know I have feelings for you too." An anxious look swept across his face as he took her hand in his.

"You don't have to say anything, Faye."

Being a detective had honed his skills, making him keenly aware of people's reactions. Had he sensed she wasn't going to tell him she loved him? Not because she didn't, but because the words didn't come easily to her. But something inside her had changed. She didn't want to hold back her love for him anymore. Looking into his eyes, she said,

"But I do have to say something." She could feel her heart beating out of her chest as he held her hand, fear clinging to the stillness in his eyes as he waited for her to speak.

"I'm in love with you, too."

They stood together in the open doorway. The moon shining in the night sky behind Tom's back fell into the hallway around them. She stepped towards him, his touch like a spark of electricity running through her as they kissed. A car screeched to a halt outside. Pemberley jumped out and came rushing towards them. He halted as if sensing he was intruding as Tom turned to him.

"Excuse me, Sir. We have a problem. Colby is kicking off. He wants to see Grace and says he's innocent."

He wiped the sweat off his brow with the back of his hand. His eyebrows dipped to meet in the middle as he said,

"He's already knocked out the desk sergeant, and it's taken three of us to drag him kicking and fighting into the cell. He's making one hell of a racket and says he won't shut up until he's spoken to you."

She could feel a silent sigh from Tom, who said,

"I'll be right there."

He turned back to her.

"Maybe tomorrow would be a better time for your statement."

Her heart sank. She didn't want him to leave. For the first time in a very long time, she felt happy.

A gentle smile creased his mouth as he held her gaze.

"I'll see you tomorrow."

Chapter Eleven
Mrs Field

A knock at the door sent Faye rushing down the hallway, half expecting Tom to be standing there. She hid her disappointment under a broad smile as she saw Gwen's beaming face.

"Gwen."

"Morning, Faye." She said, handing her the silver, foil topped milk bottle from the doorstep.

Gwen was wearing a bright red floppy bow on top of her head and a green short-sleeved dress with an apron in a cherry red and white chequered pattern over it. The red pattern was as bright as her lipstick as a smile stretched across her mouth.

"I heard about that crazy gunman last night, and I just had to come over, and to think I danced the night away with him, and all the time he could have been plotting to kill me in my bed."

Faye sighed. Gwen always had a penchant for the dramatic of any situation, which she had learnt to accept was just her way. She opened the door wide and smiled again.

"Come in, Gwen. I've just put the kettle on."

She breezed down the hallway and into the kitchen. Seeing Daniel sitting at the kitchen table stopped her in her tracks.

"Daniel. I thought you would be at work by now. Are you having a day off?"

Faye interrupted her.

"I think we could all do with a day off after yesterday."

Daniel grumbled into his teacup. "It's okay, Aunty Faye."

He glanced at Gwen.

"I'm still trying to think up an excuse for how I managed to invite a kidnapper into our company and… our most prestigious client's ball."

Gwen brushed off his remark. "Well, it's not every day you come across a kidnapper and a secret love child. You were just unlucky. And by all accounts, not as unlucky as him, now he's turned up dead."

"Do they know who killed Joe?"

She directed the question at Faye as she walked over to pick up the teapot.

"I don't know. I was expecting Tom… Inspector Rawlings to be here by now with some news."

She busied herself, not wanting to look around at Gwen, who would have noticed her cheeks flush as she tripped over Tom's name.

Gwen made herself comfortable at the kitchen table.

"They have Colby locked up in the cell. It can only have been him. He was fighting with Joe. You saw that, Faye."

Faye poured out the tea. It seemed like the obvious answer, but she couldn't know that for certain.

"I'm not so sure."

Her mind bringing up the image of Colby kneeling next to Grace.

"He seemed so in love and gentle with Grace and didn't act like a person who could murder someone."

Daniel clattered his cup down on the saucer.

"Do murderers have a certain response they use?"

She glanced at him. "You know what I mean."

Gwen stopped stirring her teacup and held the spoon in her hand.

"Love does funny things to people. Makes them act crazy."

Daniel pursed his lips. "You have personal experience?"

Faye put down her cup. "Daniel, what's got into you this morning?"

Gwen replied before Daniel had a chance.

"He's in shock. I've heard about it."

Daniel sighed as the doorbell buzzing rang out. Glad to escape, he said,

"I'll go."

But Gwen was already up and heading for the door. "You're in shock. I'll go."

He sat back down and shrugged wearily, shaking his head. Faye could hear voices at the door. Moments later, Gwen came rushing back into the kitchen.

"It's Mrs Field, and you'll never guess what."

Mrs Field's red hair came into view as she stepped past Gwen.

"It's not that dramatic, Gwen." She wriggled her shoulders, raising her nose in the air. "It was just unusual."

Faye smiled. "Mrs Field. Please take a seat. Would you like a cup of tea?"

She glanced at the tea caddy on the side. "Do you have Earl Grey?"

Daniel raised his eyes up and down at Faye, wondering if the morning could get any worse when the doorbell buzzed again. He jumped up and cast a determined eye at Gwen.

"I'll go. I need to take Buster for a walk before I go to work, anyway."

Faye followed Daniel out of the kitchen.

"Daniel. Are you okay?"

He stopped short of the door to grab his coat.

"I've got a meeting with the boss at eleven o'clock." He shuddered at the thought of going to work. "He hasn't told me why he's called the meeting, but I'm sure it has something to do with our gun-toting kidnapper."

"Oh, Daniel. I'm sure it will be fine. He can't blame you. You couldn't have known who he was."

The doorbell buzzed again.

"I guess not." He said, opening the front door.

"Inspector."

Faye noticed Tom quickly take his hat off as Buster bounded into view. Daniel grabbed Buster's lead and nodded to Tom as he rushed out the door with Buster, who was bouncing down the path.

Tom raised an eyebrow and glanced at Faye. "Everything okay?"

She felt her heart jump. Their moonlight kiss ran across her mind. Her cheeks burned as she tried to push the image out of her head.

"Yes. But I'm glad to have some sanity again now you are here. I'm afraid I have a full kitchen. Gwen and Mrs Field are here." His back stiffened at the mention of Mrs Field's name.

"Ah. Well, in that case, I'll come by later."

Gwen stuck her head out of the kitchen doorway. "Tom. You might want to hear what Mrs Field has to say."

A flash of disappointment crossed his face as he pursed his lips, debating whether to stay.

Faye smiled. "Perhaps you should hear her out?"

He sighed, his mouth tense, as he nodded and followed her down the hall.

Mrs Field could have killed Tom where he stood with the icy glare he was greeted with. Never forgiving him for wrongly arresting her for her neighbour Dolly's murder. She avowed one day to avenge the trauma he had put her through. But today, Gwen had asked her to share what she knew. Avoiding Tom's gaze, she looked at Faye.

"I saw a man in the fields by my cottage. He said he was looking for his lost dog, but I didn't recognise him from around here, and I know just about everyone in the village." She lifted her shoulders up and shook her head.

"I wouldn't normally mention it, but it was the same day that the murder took place. And as that young man is locked up, we wouldn't want to go accusing the wrong person."

She sniffed and turned her nose up, away from Tom. Faye tried to lighten the mood.

"Do you have any reports of a missing dog inspector?"

He glanced over at Mrs Field. Her arms were folded, and her face still tilted up away from him as he looked back at Faye.

"Not that I am aware of. But I can check." He gritted his jaw as he turned to Mrs Field again.

"Mrs Field, are you able to describe the man you saw?"

He watched as her tightly closed mouth twitched with irritation.

Still not facing him, she raised her head.

"Yes. I'm very good with faces."

"He wasn't very tall, only about five foot seven or so. He was in his late fifties. Quite a handsome man, by all accounts. He had a tanned face and greying hair, which was quite full for his age."

She looked to the side as she thought, then back at Faye.

"What I thought was strange was the way he jumped back from the cottage window as though he didn't want to be seen."

Gwen couldn't keep quiet any longer, caught up in the excitement of the unfolding drama.

"It must have been Joe. The man who kidnapped Grace. He wanted to take her by surprise. So, he hid before she could see him."

Faye shook her head.

"No. Joe didn't know where Grace was. That's why he came here, so he could find her." A shiver ran down her spine as the memory of Joe pointing the gun at her came flooding back.

"He may just be an innocent man who really was looking for his dog?"

From the silence in the room, Faye realised they were all grasping at straws. She looked over at Tom.

"Your job is quite a difficult one, Inspector."

Mrs Field snorting made Faye turn to her. She had been shamed in front of the entire village, in particular, the ladies of the Women's Institute, which she had been chair lady of but had to step down in light of her public arrest, and never redeemed her position. Her wrath was palpable still. Tom didn't respond. Choosing to focus on the facts before him.

"The way I see it, it couldn't be Joe. The man you are describing, Mrs Field, is too old to be Joe."

Mrs Field's cursory glance at him clearly confirmed her belief that he was a fool.

"I was held at gunpoint by Joe. It's obviously not him, as I said. I have a good eye for faces, and Joe was in his late twenties."

Gwen sat upright in her chair. "That's right. I danced with him at the manor ball. He didn't look much older than twenty-five, maybe? Her eyes lit up. Who on earth is this mystery man?" She gasped as an idea hit her.

"I'm going to ask around the village if anyone knows anything about him or a missing dog."

She lifted her China teacup and screwed her face up at the last gulp of lukewarm tea, which made her shudder.

"Right. I've got to get back to the bakery."

Mrs Field glared at Tom. "I'm leaving too. Thank you for the tea, Faye."

Faye managed a half smile, "You are welcome."

Gwen's eyes flicked over to Tom and then to Faye with a hint of delight.

"I'll leave you two in peace, then."

She left with Mrs Field trotting down the hallway behind her. Faye heard the front door shut and looked at

Tom, the silence tense. It felt like she was starting over every time she met Tom again. Her heart, on a roller coaster of emotions as she looked at him. His mouth curved into that reassuring smile that made her drop her defences.

"I want to take you out tonight."

Her heart jolted at the thought of going out in the village.

"Somewhere quiet. Without prying eyes." He said as if reading her mind. He held her gaze, waiting.

"What do you think?".

"Yes," was all she could say. Her mind seemed to go blank as he moved nearer to her.

He pushed a wavy lock of auburn hair back from her face.

"I'll pick you up at seven."

He turned to walk out and looked back. "Oh. And make sure you wear shoes for walking."

Like a giddy teenager, she couldn't help the smile that swept across her face as she watched him skip out down the step.

Chapter Twelve
Elizabeth

Faye had just started collecting half-drunk cups of tea from the kitchen table when the doorbell buzzed out again. Daniel crossed her mind. He had rushed out so quickly and probably forgotten his key. She put the cups down again and quickly went to answer the door. As she opened the door, she couldn't hide the surprise in her voice.

"Elizabeth!"

Elizabeth was wearing a very dowdy, plain grey trench coat and a large grey hat that overshadowed her face. Still wearing her red lipstick and blue eyeshadow, she looked up from beneath the hat and whispered under her breath.

"I'm in disguise. May I come in?"

Intrigued, a broad smile curved Faye's mouth. "Please do."

She stepped back as Elizabeth rushed past her. Her expensive perfume lingered in the air as Faye shut the door. Elizabeth was staring at the cups and saucers still strewn across the kitchen table as Faye caught her up.

"Oh. I was just clearing those away."

She rushed forward in a fluster, gathering up the cups and saucers.

"Please take a seat."

Elizabeth pulled out a chair and sat down as Faye placed the wobbling stack of plates and cups she had collected down on the sink.

"It's not my usual morning. But after the ordeal yesterday with..." She stopped short before mentioning Grace's name.

Elizabeth feigned her lack of care with a dismissive hand.

"You don't have to protect my feelings, darling. I fear it's all too late for that now."

Her head lowered slightly as she sighed. Faye could feel how fragile and vulnerable she was. Her usual sparkling blue eyes dulled, her face had an expression of weariness, and her familiar, upbeat spirit was gone. She put the kettle back on as Elizabeth fidgeted in her coat. It was ill-fitting and not the kind of tailored coat she was used to. She saw Faye glance over at her and looked down at the coat.

"I borrowed this from the cook. It's really rather uncomfortable."

Faye nodded in silence, wondering how long it must have taken the cook to save up for the coat. Elizabeth's diamond ring glinted as she placed her hand flat on the table to turn towards her.

"I hope you don't mind this impromptu visit, darling, but as you were there at the time of Grace's outburst, I feel I could share something with you. As I know you to be most trustworthy and highly regarded in the village."

Faye placed a fresh, steaming pot of tea on the table. Her cheeks flushed as she sat down.

"Thank you. That's very kind of you to say."

She was glad only Elizabeth was there at the table as she was sure Gwen would have something to say about that as a vision of Tom flashed in her mind.

"Well, darling. After that awful business at the ball, I..."

She stopped and reached inside her bag, pulling out a handkerchief with a blue 'E. P' beautifully monogrammed into the corner surrounded by scrolls and green leaves. She dabbed under her eyes.

"I have to come clean with George. And I don't know how to tell him."

She burst into tears, and Faye felt her stomach drop. She was about to share a secret she really didn't want to know, but seeing the usually flamboyant Elizabeth reduced to tears, she reached over and took her hand.

"George is a kind man. I'm sure he will understand."

Elizabeth nodded to herself.

"Yes. Yes. He is."

Faye lifted her hand from Elizabeth's as she straightened up.

"I haven't spoken to anyone about Grace." Her name caught in her throat, and she coughed.

"Not since the ball. That's why I'm dressed in this awful..." She glanced at her coat. "Rag. "I'm reduced to hiding in the shadows dressed like a pauper."

Her lips closed tightly together as her face became stern.

"Well, I'm not doing it any longer. Florence be damned."

She stood up.

"Faye. I need your help." Desperation flooded her eyes as she stared at her.

"Yes. Of course."

"Thank you, darling. Can you meet me at the Manor House tomorrow morning?"

Faye wanted to make an excuse to keep out of the drama but thought better of it as Elizabeth's pleading eyes connected with her. She drew in a breath and released it.

"Yes. What did you have in mind?"

"Oh, it's all very simple. Just be prompt. Say ten o'clock."

A smile lit up Elizabeth's face as she made for the door. "I'll see myself out. Thank you, darling. See you tomorrow at ten o'clock sharp."

She swept down the hallway and out the Station House door. Faye leant back in her chair in the now silent kitchen, wondering what on earth she had let herself in for.

Chapter Thirteen
Young and Spirited

The familiar sound of the cell door slamming echoed out behind Inspector Rawlings. He had managed to calm Colby down by assuring him Grace was safe and left the cell, aware he couldn't keep him in custody without evidence for much longer. He rolled his shirtsleeves up and walked down the corridor into the interview room. Grace sat motionless, her face blank - hands clasped together. To an untrained eye, her calm demeanour would have fooled most. Her foot tapped nervously on the floor as he sat down opposite her, aware the silence was uncomfortable for her. She was young and spirited, and he immediately thought of Elizabeth, her bright blue eyes shining back at him as she looked up, agitated.

"Where is Colby? Is he okay?"

"He's in custody right now. And perfectly okay."

Her eyes darted to the door and back.

"I want to see him...Please," she pleaded.

His eyes narrowed, thinking, as he stared at her. Her desperate need to speak with Colby was a weakness, and he could use it as a bartering tool to coax out the truth from her. He picked up the pen and paper lying on top of a file on the desk and pushed it towards her.

"First things first. What is your full name?"

Her mouth pulled back as she sighed and folded her arms, slumping back in her chair.

"I already told the other policeman; my name is Grace Wellen."

"And where do you live, Miss Wellen?"

He saw the fear in her eyes as she looked down. His hunch - she was running scared, away from someone or something.

She shook her head. "Nowhere. Not anymore."

Her voice was desperate as she looked back up at him. "Can I see Colby now? I need to know he is okay."

"Miss Wellen…Grace.".

"Please focus on the question. You have no fixed abode here? In England?"

She looked away.

"No. The first place I stayed at, was Mrs Field's."

The mention of Mrs Field set his teeth on edge as he watched Grace shift uncomfortably in her seat. She was still lying to him. He pulled the file on the desk towards him and opened it out. Taking out a photograph, he slid it across the desk towards her.

"Do you know this man?"

Horror turned to sadness in her eyes as she looked at the photograph of the lifeless body lying sprawled across the orange and brown leaves of the forest floor. Her hair had fallen forward, long and blonde. It hung straight as she tucked it behind her ear and wiped her hand across her cheeks, catching her tears.

"He was my ex-fiancé, Joe. I left him to come to England a few weeks ago. Only…"

"Yes." He urged as she paused. He wasn't immune to her sadness, but he needed to get to the truth. With a dead body and no witness, it was imperative he found out what she was hiding.

"He followed me somehow." She struggled to speak as she sobbed… "And now he's dead. But it couldn't have been Colby…" she stressed. Her eyes were red from crying as she stared at him.

"He's not like that. He's kind."

He stared coldly at her.

"Does Colby own a firearm?"

She shook her head. "No. I told you. He's not like that."

To keep asking her about Colby when she was under his spell and clearly in love with him would be a waste of his time. Faye briefly crossed his mind as he closed the cover of the file shut.

"When you were at the Manor Ball, you had blood over your coat and hands. Whose blood was it?"

She gripped her hands tightly together, her face screwed up in pain as she glanced briefly at him before lowering her head again.

"Colby's."

She shook her head.

"Joe. He wouldn't stop. He kept chasing us and shot Colby in the arm."

Her breathing became faster.

"I was so scared as I was on the ground holding Colby that I picked up a rock and threw it at him. It hit him in the side of his head, "here." She pointed to the side of her temple. "And he fell over. I got Colby up, and we ran away from him and to the Manor House."

She burst into tears, burying her face in her hands. "Colby is protecting me. I killed Joe."

He leant back in his seat.

"I can put you out of your misery there, Grace. The rock you threw didn't kill Joe, otherwise he wouldn't have been able to come back and kidnap you. He died, in fact, from a fatal gunshot wound."

She looked up, relief in her eyes.

"So, Colby and I can go, then?"

"Not just yet. Why was Joe chasing you?"

She shrugged, her hair clinging to her damp cheeks.

"Because he wouldn't let me go. I was his property. That's the way he saw it. But I couldn't do it any longer. His drinking was out of control, just like his temper."

She shuddered and drew her knees up, wrapping her arms around them as she balanced on the edge of the seat. Her chin rested on her knees as she stared blankly at the grey wall. The distress in her vacant expression took him to his own childhood, cowering in a cupboard, sitting as she was now, listening in fear for his father's footsteps, praying he wouldn't find him. He turned to Pemberley, standing by the door.

"Pemberley, can you get a cup of tea and a sandwich for Miss Wellen?"

"Right, you are, sir."

Pemberley shot off out the door as he turned back to Grace.

"You said you have only been in England for a few weeks. How did you get here?"

She slowly lifted her head and placed her feet back on the floor again.

"I came by ship."

A smile stretched across her closed mouth.

"That's where I met Colby."

He sighed, not sure if she was ready to hear what he was about to say.

"Grace, Colby is a wanted man back home in America... for rape."

He watched her as she looked away and then back.

"I know. His ex-girlfriend is lying. She accused him of it because he broke up with her. She wanted to get back at him."

"That's as maybe, but he has to go back and face the charges."

Her face dropped, crestfallen. She looked away.

"Where did you go when you got off the ship?"

He paused when she didn't reply.

"It's a long way from the docks to Petworth. You have to have stayed somewhere."

As if resigned to her fate, she sighed and told him about Ned and the first house they stayed in and their journey to the farmhouse. She smiled as she recounted the kindness of Reg, the farmer, and his wife, Cathy, and their train journey to Petworth. By the time Pemberley arrived with sandwiches and tea, he was writing down the last of her statement. She had done what he had asked and told him everything she knew and was now staring intently at him.

"When can I see Colby?"

He stood up and gathered the file together.

"Tomorrow."

He knew she wouldn't move far away from where Colby was and saw no need to detain her any longer.

"You are free to go. Please leave details of where we can contact you with Officer Pemberley."

He checked his watch. He had an hour. Just enough time to go home and get ready before he had to leave to pick up Faye. His stomach flitted with nervous excitement at the thought of holding Faye in his arms again. And with a spring in his step, he walked hastily out the door.

Chapter Fourteen
Glenda

Faye felt a rush of excitement tingle up her spine when she heard Tom knock on the door at exactly seven o'clock. Ready to go in her flat shoes and thick, warm coat, she opened the door. His eyes traced down to her shoes, smiling in appreciation of her readiness. He looked back at her, but she noticed a hint of apprehension in his glance as he smiled and held out his arm for her to take.

As they walked past his Humber sat outside, he noticed her turn and said,

"It's not far. Just a short walk."

He was acting slightly odd as he avoided her gaze, and an unsettled feeling bubbled up inside her stomach. But she trusted him and relaxed as they walked past white cottages with a faint light coming through the windows, spilling onto the path. Under the moonlight, the trees formed shadows that arched over towards the middle of the road as the village took on a mysterious life of its own. They walked in silence until they reached the duck pond. Tom took his arm from hers and stopped, turning towards her.

"Faye. I need to talk to you."

His frown deepened as he stared at her. His throat dipped as he struggled to find the words. Her own anxiety silenced her as she waited for him to say what he was struggling with. Her mind took over, imagining all sorts of scenarios. Was he going to say he didn't love her? That it had all been a mistake? She caught her breath as he spoke.

"Faye. I want to take you to meet my mother."

She let out a gasp of air, mostly relief but also surprise. She smiled back at him, trying to allay his nervousness. Wondering why it was such a big deal for him to ask her.

"I would love to meet her."

He paused, still frowning.

"She's been unwell for a long time."

She recognised the pain in his eyes. The feeling of hopelessness that comes when there is nothing you can do to help.

"Oh, Tom. I'm so sorry."

His head bent, he nodded.

"I've had a while to adjust. It's just… she's taken a turn for the worst this week."

His eyes became vacant as he bit his lip, fighting to stop the tears from spilling down his face.

"She doesn't move much out of her bed now."

Her heart sank, seeing him so distraught. An image of her father flashed in her mind. Bedridden for weeks before he passed, she had spent every day reading and talking and looking at old photographs and laughing at the way their hair was styled then. They were some of her happiest memories with him, but it didn't take the pain away when he finally passed over. She reached out and took Tom's hand in hers.

"When my father was ill, I spent as much time as I could with him. I know it made him happy. I'm sure your mother will appreciate you taking the time to visit her."

He nodded, and they continued walking in a shared silence of understanding until they arrived at the last cottage on the road. It was tiny and a little ramshackle, even in the moonlight. The front garden was burgeoning with last year's overgrown shrubs that spilt over the picket fence and onto the gate as they walked down the path. The cottage door wasn't locked, and Tom turned the handle and swung it open. In complete contrast to the wayward front garden, the small room they entered was immaculate. Two green armchairs were on either side of the fireplace, and a crackling fire in the hearth gave the room a soft glow. A white, bowl-shaped lamp shone out as it sat on top of a doily on the side table next to a brown and cream, porcelain shire horse.

"Tom!"

A stout woman in her early fifties wearing black rimmed glasses and tight grey curls strangely resembling her old school teacher, stood beaming at Tom. She kissed him on his cheek and looked behind him towards her.

"You must be Faye. I'm Rita, Tom's aunt."

Faye held out her hand, but she brushed it away and drew her into a hug, kissing her on the cheek.

"We're informal here." She said as she released her.

Gwen came to mind, and she wondered if it was a family trait to hug everyone.

"Come in. Come in."

She ushered them forward as she closed the door behind them.

"I've just put the kettle on."

She glanced at Tom. Her smile faded as she lowered her voice.

"Glenda is awake. She's had a tough day."

A knowing look passed between them before she disappeared under the crooked wooden beam of the doorway that led to the kitchen. Tom's tension was palpable as he took his coat off and hung it on the back of the cottage door. Following his lead, she hung her coat up on the hook next to his. He turned as if to speak and paused. She could feel him tense up as he looked at her. He was still concerned about taking her in. She took his hand and, squeezing it in silent acknowledgement, smiled at him. The uneven floorboards groaned underfoot, creaking like old age had set in its bones as they walked to the stairs. Each threadbare step they trod on continued to creak until they reached the top. Off to the right, a light fell through a gap in the doorway. Tom pushed the door open and called out.

"Mum. It's me. And I have Faye with me."

A swell of happiness rose in her chest. Tom had already told his mother about her. Still a little on edge, she trod softly behind him, only stepping to the side of him as they reached the end of the bed. A heavy, pale blue, flowery eiderdown quilt cradled the bed, obscuring her face as she lay facing the wall away from them. She stirred and looked up. Her grey hair was flat against her frail features.

"Tom."

She tried to sit up, and he rushed to her side, putting his arm behind her, lifting her until her back was steady against her pillow. Her hand faltered, trembling as she went to lift it. Tears stung his eyes as she gasped for breaths between words.

"Thank you for coming. I know how busy you are."

He sat carefully on the side of the bed and took her hand. Faye's stomach lurched seeing the bones on Glenda's arms and hands were so thin and fragile, as though at the slightest movement, they could snap like a twig. Gravely ill, she wondered if she was clinging on for a little longer to see Tom, and he had sensed it, too. She could feel Tom's eyes looking at her, noticing her shock. She smiled, softly reassuring him, and reached over to Glenda.

"I'm Faye. And I'm so pleased to meet you."

The sound of teacups and saucers rattling grew closer, and she was grateful for Rita's presence, breaking the tension as she finally emerged in the doorway carrying a tray fully laden with teapot and milk jug, cups balanced on saucers and biscuits on a China plate. Tom sprung up.

"Let me get that, Aunty."

Sweat glistened on her brow as she thanked Tom, relieved to be free of the burgeoning heavy tray. Faye stepped back and found a small pink velvet stool under the dressing table and pulled it out to sit just a little way back from Tom at the end of the bed. Rita sat on an old wooden chair on the opposite side as Tom chatted about Gwen and the bakery, and his mother seemed blissfully happy to listen as she leaned back, a smile drawn across her mouth. Tom stood up and leaned over her as she whispered in his ear. He smiled, looking at Faye as she handed him a tea. Her stomach rose in a whirl of butterflies, and she felt strangely coy at the look of happiness in his eyes. By the end of the evening, she had laughed at the many stories of escaping chickens and the antics of the farm dog that couldn't be trained, making her feel like she had lived through those times with them. As they said their goodbyes, Glenda took Faye's hand.

"I think you and Tom are going to be very happy."

Faye blushed and looked away. Aware of Tom's gaze upon her.

Glenda beckoned Tom over as she let Faye's hand slip from hers, and Faye's heart dropped as she saw how weak and limp, she had become. It may be the only time she would have with her, but her heart was glad Tom had trusted in her to share their precious time together.

The walk back to the Station House was mostly in silence. The image of Glenda's frail body hung unspoken between them as they reached the gate and walked down the moonlit path. Daniel had left a light on for her, softly falling on the evergreen leaves of the roses climbing around the outside of the door. She reached for her key when she felt the gentle pull of Tom's hand in hers, guiding her under the shadow of the apple tree. Longing filled his eyes as he held her, moving a wisp of hair back from her face.

"Faye." He whispered as she felt the warmth of his arms wrapped around her. Her breath caught as he pressed his lips to hers, claiming her heart in the silence of the night.

Love And Murder At The Manor
Chapter Fifteen
Elizabeth

Faye rushed around, looking for her scarf. Time had escaped her this morning. Her heart still full of happiness as she pondered her moonlight kiss with Tom under the apple tree. She smiled to herself as Buster nudged her leg and went and sat by his bowl, staring back at her. Daniel lumbered into the kitchen yawning and glanced at Buster and then to Faye.

"I see Buster has his priorities right. Breakfast first."

He watched Faye pulling out a cushion, still searching for her scarf.

"I'll feed him. And I think you'll find what you're looking for over there."

He nodded towards Buster's bed. A bright pink scarf poking out from under the grey blanket.

"Oh, Buster. What on earth are you playing at?"

She marched over and picked up her scarf, sighing as she saw the slobber and muddy teeth marks clinging to the corner.

"I can't wear that now."

Daniel shook Buster's biscuits into his bowl and looked up.

"Are you going somewhere important?"

"Yes and no."

His eyes lit up. "That sounds mysterious."

She pulled her mouth to one side and bit the inside of her lip. Annoyed at herself for piquing Daniel's interest, which was the last thing she needed, after promising to keep Elizabeth's visit a secret. Not that she liked secrets and didn't want to keep any, especially from Daniel. But he would ask more questions if she didn't share something with him, and at least he wouldn't go gossiping around the village like Gwen would if she were here now.

"Not really. Elizabeth has asked me over to the Manor." She shrugged. A frown formed across her brow.

"I'm not sure why. Other than she wants me to be there when she speaks to George."

Daniel took the milk bottle out of the fridge and reached for the blue-and-white striped breakfast bowl.

"No prizes for guessing what it's about. Grace is obviously Elizabeth's illegitimate daughter. You only have to look at her to see she's the spitting image of her."

Faye didn't reply. She had thought the same thing.

"Is Inspector Rawlings going to be there? As you are a couple now."

He grinned as she blushed.

"Wherever did you hear that?"

He poured the cornflakes into a bowl and said nonchalantly.

"Gwen might have mentioned it. And for the record. I think you two make a perfect couple."

He smiled and looked up at her. It was pointless to object. Daniel had a nose for flushing out the truth, and given that Gwen had now probably let it slip to the entire village, she resigned herself to her fate and smiled back with a nod. Buster, picking up his bowl and clanging it on the floor, interrupted them.

"I'll walk him before I go to work… Take his mind off looking for more food."

"You haven't lost your job then?" She said, relieved.

He rolled his eyes upward and gasped.

"Thank the lord. No. I only got a rap on the knuckles. But Edmund moving a big account of his from *Ticklers* to our firm was a winner and saved my bacon."

He whistled to himself, no doubt as relieved as she was. Faye would not have let him struggle financially. She had more than enough from her mother's estate, which was a shock finding out her mother had left her fortune to her as she had always professed; she was going to leave it to the cats' home. But in a moment of kindness, she must have changed her mind, and Faye was thankful for that. But it was more about Daniel's pride in himself. He had lost several jobs in the past, and he needed this one to find a sense of normality again. A few minutes later, and still whistling, Daniel headed out the door with Buster.

"See you tonight. Don't let the bedbugs bite."

The door slammed shut, and Faye followed on his heels, heading out for the hour-long walk to the Manor. The sun broke through the clouds as she arrived, but the Manor House looked just as imposing in the daylight as it did at night. Mottled, grey stone gargoyles with bat-like wings and fangs grinned down at her from the corbels above, and she trod uneasily up the steps, passing through ornately carved, white, marble pillars on either side of the huge wooden front door. She lifted the black iron ring groaning on rusty hinges and knocked on the door, its weight reverberating through her hand as it hammered out loudly around her. Footsteps behind her made her turn. Her heart jumped at the sight of Tom.

He was just as surprised to see her as he bounced up the steps and stared at her, a frown creasing his forehead as she said,

"Tom. What are you doing here?"

His jaw tensed.

"I could ask you the same question."

Concern softened his eyes as he stepped closer to her.

"Faye. I need to know you are safe and not getting mixed up in any unsavoury business."

He turned his head to take in the surrounding doorway of the Manor and sighed before looking back at her. She felt the heckles go up on the back of her neck. She didn't need Tom wrapping her up in cotton wool. Indignation rose in her voice.

"I'm not getting mixed up in anything. Elizabeth has asked me to come here."

Unsure why and thinking of a reasonable explanation, she paused… "To help her…. speak to Edmund."

He stiffened his back, "I see."

She seized the opportunity to divert his attention from her.

"What about you?"

He twisted around to look at his car and she stared, open mouthed as Grace closed the car door behind her.

"I'm bringing Grace here at Elizabeth's request.

Elizabeth's plan became clearer to her now that she had seen Grace. A nauseous feeling swept over her as she thought of Elizabeth, Edmund and Grace, all in the same room together. The front door suddenly creaked open, and Faye drew in a breath, hoping it would all go as smoothly as Elizabeth seemed to think it would.

Chapter Sixteen
Grace

As they stood in the stately dining room, Faye shivered with cold and glanced over to the dying embers of the fire. A stack of logs piled up in the fireplace, ready for the evening gathering, was being tended to by a young girl, who quickly poked the blackened pieces of burnt wood, sending sparks shooting up, then balanced logs in a crisscross fashion over them, before scuttling out the room. A mounting sense of foreboding filled her as they waited for Elizabeth to appear. She folded her arms across her body as Tom glanced her way.

"They don't hold the heat, these big rooms."

The corner of her mouth curved up as she nodded, nonchalantly looking around, taking in the huge gold framed paintings hanging on the walls, depicting men in battledress and women in their finery.

As she studied the red uniform and sword held in one hand of the uniformed man. Edmund walked into the room behind her.

"A Custodian of the house before us. He was a fine upstanding officer."

She spun around as he smiled, inclining his head towards the pictures.

"My great, great grandfather Lord Percival Percy. Or Percy, Percy, as he was affectionately known."

She frowned without realising it, wondering what kind of parent would name a child so oddly when he shrugged.

"Rather an odd choice of names, but there you have it."

Elizabeth's voice commanded their attention as she swept in.

"Edmund, what utter nonsense. He was a gambler and a cheat and nearly ruined the family name."

She paused, her diamond necklace glinting, grabbing Faye's attention as the words caught in her throat. She recovered quickly and turned to greet her.

"Faye darling." She kissed her on both cheeks.

"And Inspector Rawlings." She dipped her head in acknowledgement.

Edmund's ruddy cheeks, like polished tomatoes, drew Faye's eye as he took Tom's hand and shook it.

"To what do we owe this pleasure? Nothing serious, I hope."

His laugh had an undertone of nervousness about it, made worse as he stared in shock at Grace, emerging from behind the library wall, which was a blind spot in the room. Elizabeth's voice cut through the tension as it carried across the open space. She opened her arms out to Grace as she spoke.

"Grace darling. Thank you for coming."

She turned to Faye and Tom.

"Thank you all for coming this morning."

She placed her hand in Edmund's and squeezed it tightly, smiling at him.

Utter bewilderment clung to his widening eyes as he stared at her.

"What on earth is going on, Lizzy?"

With a slight nod of her head in Tom's direction, she said,

"I've asked the inspector to come along with Grace and Faye."

Faye could see underneath Elizabeth's broadening smile, the worry in her eyes as she turned back to Edmund.

"To clarify a few things from the other night."

Edmund jumped in, cutting her off.

"Surely, it's all water under the bridge. Just a mistake. The poor girl was delirious."

She raised her chin up to stand her ground.

"No, Edmund. You need to hear this, and so does Grace."

Elizabeth's furtive glance towards her before she addressed Grace made her stomach drop as she waited for the undoubted bombshell to descend on them all.

"Grace, darling. I'm not your mother."

Faye let out a sigh of relief and wondered why on earth she had asked them all there.

Edmund raised up his shoulders as he stared at Elizabeth.

"Right. Well, I'm glad that's been sorted. No need to drag it out, Lizzy."

Faye was inclined to agree with him, as Elizabeth said,

"Edmund. Please."

Her face was unusually drawn and serious, silencing him.

"It's not all sorted. In fact, it's far from sorted."

Anxiety got the better of her as she glanced at Edmund and wrung her hands together in an unusual display of nerves. Then, she walked over to the silver tray sitting on the long side cabinet and poured herself a sherry. The chinking of glass rang out as she put the stopper back on the decanter. Taking a huge swig, she placed the glass on the table.

She inhaled a deep breath and turned to him. "Edmund. Grace is your sister."

Edmund's jowls drooped down under his chin as his mouth opened. He stammered his words as he briefly glanced at Grace and back to Elizabeth.

"That's…. That's preposterous."

He rushed over to the side cabinet and poured a whisky. Faye noticed his hands trembling as he lifted the glass to his lips. He peered over the rim of the glass and realizing all eyes were upon him, straightened up and looked at Tom.

"Where are my manners? Inspector, Faye, would you care for a glass of something?"

She noticed he hadn't included Grace and was avoiding looking her way as Tom shook his head.

"Not for me, thank you. I'm on duty."

She felt taking a drink would help both Elizabeth and Edmund feel less self-conscious.

"Thank you, Edmund. Just a small sherry, please."

Elizabeth's face had gone pale as she turned back to him.

"I thought it was for the best that you knew."

Grace was wide-eyed as she stared first at Edmond and then Elizabeth, who managed a faint smile towards her and said.

"I'm sorry, darling, but it's complicated."

Although Grace looked composed on the outside, the slight tremble in her voice betrayed her.

"But if you aren't my mom, who is?"

For the first time, Elizabeth seemed to crumble, reaching out for the top of the dining room chair to steady herself. Tom quickly pulled out the chair next to her, guiding her into the seat.

"Edmund. Darling."

She held out her hand to Edmund, who, still visibly shaken, walked over and stood by her. Patting his hand in hers, she looked up at him.

"I'm sorry, darling. But Madeline is Grace's mother."

The glass in his hand dropped to the floor, bouncing and shattering into a million pieces as if in slow motion across the wooden parquet tiles, some landing under the window, glinting in the sunlight.

Edmond's voice bellowed out, making Faye jump.

"Good God! Are you saying… that my father had an affair...and Grace…?"

His attention turned to Grace as Elizabeth's eyes darted towards him like a frightened animal as she grappled to find the right words.

"Yes. Your father had an affair…with my mother… There. I've said it."

She reached inside her pocket and pulled out her handkerchief and dabbed under her eyes before looking over at Grace.

"And you, my darling. Are their love child."

Grace's mouth fell open as she stared at Elizabeth.

"So, you…and Edmund…are my brother and sister?"

Elizabeth nodded.

"Yes, darling."

Grace paused,

"And Madeline, your mother, is…?"

"Yes, darling. Your mother, too."

Relief filled Elizabeth's smile as she said,

"You have her eyes."

Faye could see Grace's legs start to buckle under her and ran, catching her arm just in time. She walked her to the highbacked chair and sat her down. Tom ran a hand through his hair as he turned to Elizabeth.

"I need to know if Grace will be staying here with you. In case I need to speak with her?"

Edmund cleared his throat.

"I think Grace deserves that much."

She had been right about Edmund's kindness. He had already adjusted to the unfolding events, and Faye breathed a sigh of relief, glad the worst part was over, aware it could have gone so much worse.

Tom grabbed his hat from the table.

"Grace. You are still part of an ongoing murder investigation. Please stay in Petworth and let me know if you decide to leave the village."

Elizabeth stood up.

"I'll make sure she is well cared for here, Inspector. She is family, after all."

Tom nodded.

"Right. I'll be off then."

He glanced at Faye.

"Do you require a ride home, Miss Lantern?"

She could see the rain falling down through the window and smiled at him.

"Thank you, Inspector. I would appreciate a lift back."

Elizabeth rushed over to Faye.

"Thank you so much for your assistance today, darling. You must come over for lunch next week so I can thank you properly."

Faye didn't feel she had helped at all and was still wondering why Elizabeth had asked her there. But she wanted to go home, and smiled back, knowing it was the easiest thing to do in that situation.

"Of Course. That would be lovely."

Relieved to be free of the unfolding drama, Faye got into the car with Tom.

"Poor Edmund. He was so surprised. Elizabeth certainly has a lot more explaining to do… to both of them. It was a big secret to keep from him."

Tom drove quickly out through the Manor House gates.

"She had her reasons, no doubt."

Faye noticed the car seemed to move quicker and quicker past the trees and hedgerow and looked over at him.

"Are you in a rush?"

"I have a lead in the case. I need to get back to look at the evidence."

"Oh." Is that to do with Joe's death?"

He nodded. She was eager to hear more, but his silence told her he wouldn't divulge the details to her about an ongoing investigation. As they pulled up at the Station House, he sighed.

"At least I know where Grace will be if I need to speak with her."

She smiled.

"I'm just glad she has been accepted into the family, and she is not on her own."

She noticed Tom staring at her, a gentleness in his eyes as she looked questioningly at him. He didn't move his gaze.

"You are always so understanding and kind. I wish more people thought the way you do."

She wasn't used to praise. It made her feel uncomfortable, but she resisted the urge to bat away his words like she usually did. He leaned towards her, taking her hand.

"I have to take a trip tomorrow to check on something. When I get back, I would like to see you...to ask you something."

With his eyes focused on her, her heart pounded as she caught her breath. Was it possible? Was he going to propose to her? As casually as she could, she said.

"Okay."

He let her hand go, and a smile curved his mouth.

"I'll pick you up at eight o'clock."

She got out of the car and watched him drive away. Her heart still racing.

Love And Murder At The Manor
Chapter Seventeen
An Unexpected Liaison

Tom felt inside his jacket pocket, his fingers reaching for the small velvet box containing his mother's engagement ring she had given to him after meeting Faye. He felt a rush of warmth wash over him, and the image of Faye smiling and her blushing face appeared in his mind. Whistling, he tried to dampen down a blonde wave on the top of his head. Patting it down without success as it sprang back up. He sighed. His hair seemed to have a mind of its own. Checking his watch, he headed for the door. He was keen to arrive on time, and running to his car, jumped in and drove at speed, rehearsing the words he wanted to say to her in his mind. Ten minutes later, he pulled up outside the Station House. His eyes scanned the outside of the building. The curtains were drawn, and no visible light came from the windows. He jumped out of the car and walked up the path. His mind questioned every detail of the house, which was now something inherent in him from working as an inspector, and he couldn't switch it off even if he wanted to.

He walked past the apple tree bathed in moonlight and smiled to himself, the thought of Faye in his arms again, the smell of her perfume filling his senses, as he hovered at the front door before knocking. He heard Buster's bark from somewhere inside, then steps quickly approaching from the hallway. As the door opened, his face dropped.

"Daniel."

Raising his hands up, Daniel glanced at him, a curve raising the side of his mouth.

"Don't worry. I'm not your date, Inspector. Faye left strict instructions to tell you she was at the George and Dragon. She's meeting a man there."

Tom felt his heart jolt.

"A Man?"

Daniel nodded.

"Yes. It's all perfectly innocent. Apparently, he is Grace and Colby's friend. A farmer, I think. They met on their travels here."

Tom's heart raced as panic flooded through his body. He turned and ran down the path and out the gate, leaving Daniel standing with a look of bewilderment on his face.

"You're welcome." He called out. Shaking his head, as he shut the Station House door behind him.

As the door to the George and Dragon flew open, Faye's face lit up as she saw Tom walk in. He was out of breath, frantically looking around the room. She leant in and mouthed to Reg,

"That's Inspector Rawlings… Tom." Her mouth curved into a smile. "My date I told you about. I'll go over to him and let him know where we are sitting."

His eyes, dark against greying hair and tanned, weathered skin, shifted to Tom and back as he raised his glass of ale to take a sip.

"Okay, Lass."

She weaved her way through the team of men holding darts in one hand and pints of beer in the other until she reached Tom. Unable to hear above the roar of laughter as the men greeted each other in excited anticipation of the darts tournament, she raised her voice.

"Tom. Sorry for the change in plans. Did Daniel explain to you about Reg?"

Relief spread across his face. He didn't reciprocate her smile as his eyes darted behind her, scanning the crowd. He rushed an arm around her shoulder, as he guided her back outside. She had no idea what was going on as he relaxed his grip on her shoulder and stared at her, his eyes full of panic.

"Faye."

Confused, she stared blankly at him.

"Tom. What is going on?"

"The man you were sitting and drinking with is Reg Tanner, and he's wanted by the police."

Faye could hardly take in what he was saying. It didn't fit with the kind man she was talking with. She frowned, wondering why he was wanted by the police as she looked back at Tom, trying to make sense of the situation.

"But he seems such a …fragile and sweet man."

Tom didn't move his gaze away from her, his eyes fixed intently as he frowned.

"That's as, maybe. But I have to take him into custody."

He glanced at the street, bathed in moonlight.

"Can you make your way home by yourself?"

Part of her felt a sense of pride swell up in her chest. Tom trusted she could take care of herself. But her reasoning kept her feet firmly fixed to the ground where she stood.

"Yes. But I'm not going to. He is a perfectly harmless, and kind, man."

Tom's frustration showed on his face as beads of sweat formed on his brow.

"Faye. This is not a game. He could be highly dangerous."

She went to argue, tossing her hair back as a burly man walked past her, and opened the pub door just as a loud cheer from the darts players rang out. She ducked inside, Tom just missing catching hold of her elbow. The men were thinning out as a game ended, and Faye hastily made her way through the stragglers, still ordering beer at the bar, until she found the table she left Reg at.

Tom was directly behind her as she turned. Frustration burned in his eyes, and a pang of guilt swept over her. She hadn't meant to upset him. She shrugged.

"He's gone."

Tom scanned the room before turning back to her.

"I need to call this in and get help. Stay here...Please." He stressed.

Reluctantly, she sat down and watched him disappear behind the bar. The landlord directed him towards the telephone, and a few minutes later, he reappeared and rushed over to her.

"I've contacted the station. They are searching for Turner now."

He pulled a notepad and pencil from his coat pocket and sat down next to her. He remembered her artwork hanging on the Station House walls and held out the notepad and pencil.

"Could you draw his face? For my officers to get an impression of what he looks like? Including what he was wearing."

She took the notepad and quickly sketched Reg's face with ease, adding laughter lines and the kindness in his eyes that she had seen. Handing it back to him, she stood up as Pemberley came rushing in.

"I may go home, after all, Tom. I'll use the ladies' entrance to leave at the side."

He jumped up and walked with her outside.

"I'm not leaving you alone until you are safely back home."

His face creased into a hardened look, and she knew it would be pointless to argue with him.

As they reached the Station House, Tom waited until she had stepped into the hallway. With one hand on the door, ready to close it, he hesitated, and she could see a look of frustration cross his face.

"Is everything okay, Tom?"

He stepped into the hallway, his face softening.

"Faye... I..."

He reached inside his jacket pocket when a loud whistle pierced the air, making him spin around. Out of the darkness, Pemberley came running down the road at full pelt, and skidded, turning into a narrow lane. Tom span back around, dropping his hand from his pocket.

"I have to go."

She reached out, putting her hand on his arm.

"Please be careful."

He held her gaze for a moment, his face softening, before fleeing down the steps, running to catch up with Pemberley.

Chapter Eighteen
Reg

It was a good deal after lunch that Faye walked Buster down to the canal. She admired the changing colours of the trees lining the banks of the river as autumn took hold, splashing the bright orange and gold hues of leaves against the crisp blue skies. Buster seemed to enjoy the duck's company, who had grown used to their weekly visits, and their waddle began to turn into an unexpectedly fast run as they saw Faye and Buster approach. She was about to walk back along the lane when she heard a voice calling her name.

"Cooeee. Faye."

She turned to see Mrs Fields rushing towards her, out of breath. Sweat ran down her forehead as her red hair clung to her brow. Gasping for air, she stopped and bent forwards, taking a few deep breaths in and out, waving her hand at Faye to wait a moment. Gathering herself together, she straightened up.

"Oh. Faye. You really must come to my cottage this instant."

Her face was unusually joyous as she clasped her hands together with excitement.

"It's such good news."

Her eyes were bulging and looked fit to burst as she stared, waiting for her to reply. Mrs Field's cat Peony sprung to Faye's mind. She would not let Buster into her cottage and upset her cat, but Faye didn't want to leave Buster alone outside, just in case he decided to dig an impromptu hole in her neatly manicured lawn. She felt that, in this instance, a lie would be better for all their sakes.

"Really, Mrs Field. I'm sure there is nothing so exciting it cannot wait."

Mrs Field squealed with delight, clasping her hands together.

"Oh, but there is. Come and see. Now."

She waved her hand, beckoning Faye to follow.

Faye sighed.

"I'm sorry, but I have to meet someone. It's important."

Her cheeks blushed at the barefaced lie she was telling her, but Mrs Field was undeterred and lowered her head slightly, a knowing look in her eyes.

"Not as important as this, Faye."

Faye pulled her lips back in a grimace as she ran through options to avoid taking Buster to her cottage when Mrs Field interrupted her thoughts.

"I can see you need time. Maybe tonight, then. I'll be at the George and Dragon for an hour or so. Maybe you could pop in."

An uncontrollable smile swept across her face as she said,

"I promise you won't be disappointed."

She turned and fled back along the towpath before Faye could object. With a sigh of relief that she had at least left her in peace, she began walking back, wondering what on earth had got her so worked up.

A flock of geese flying in formation, honking in the sky as they flew over her head, made her look up. As she followed their flight path across the treetops into the distance, her eyes lowered, catching sight of a man standing by the stile at the end of the hedgerow, leading into the next field. Buster let out a low grumble under his breath as she felt her heart quicken. The man began walking towards her, waving his cap. She peered at him; her eyes narrowed as she tried to make out who he was. Her sharp intake of breath as Reg came into view made Buster grumble again. Tom's lecture about how dangerous Reg could be, ran through her mind as he got closer. She noticed mud clinging to his jacket pocket, trousers, and boots. His face was weary, as though he had slept rough last night.

He stopped a short distance from her.

"I'm glad I found you, Faye. I wanted to apologise for what happened last night."

He twisted his cap anxiously in his hands as he spoke.

"But I had to leave."

Something about him seemed so gentle and comfortable to be around, and she felt her guard drop.

He inclined his head towards Buster.

"You have a fine-looking dog there."

Buster, as if sensing the same good feeling she had about him, stepped towards him, wagging his tail.

Reg's hands lowered to his sides as Faye smiled back at him.

"Yes. He is a wonderful dog, and I always trust his judgement."

His head dipped in acknowledgement as he reached out and patted Buster, rubbing his ears. After a few moments, he looked up at her. Her stomach dropped as she saw the pain in his eyes, like a defeated animal that had given up the fight.

"Do you mind if I walk aways' with you? To give me a chance to explain what happened last night."

She dismissed him and started walking.

"That's really not necessary. I'm sure you had your reasons."

He quickened his step to catch up with her.

"It won't take long."

Her mind flashed back to the portrait drawing she had done of him at the pub, and guilt racked through her.

A half smile ran across her closed mouth as she turned to him.

"Just for a minute, then."

She wondered what Tom would say after she agreed, seeing her strolling along with his prime suspect. But maybe she could learn something from him that would help Tom find out who murdered Joe. As he walked beside her, she felt an overriding urge to be honest with him.

"Mr. Turner. I think it only fair that I tell you the police are looking for you in connection with Joe's murder."

She blurted it out in a rush, her heart racing as she looked towards him. He nodded; his head lowered. A breeze blew across them, rippling up through the trees, making the leaves shiver and drop, skipping across their feet as they walked. After a few moments of silence, he stopped and raised his head to look at her.

"I had forty-two glorious years with my Cath, and now she's gone."

Tears spilt down his cheeks as he raised his head to look skyward.

"She'll be watin' for me with the kettle on, no doubt."

A smile crept along his mouth and faded away. He dropped to his knees as grief overtook him and sunk back on his haunches, then leant forward, his face in his hands. She reached out, placing a hand on his shoulder.

"I'm so sorry for your loss, Reg."

He took a moment, his breathing heavy as he wiped under his eyes with his sleeve.

"It was me, see. I shot Joe."

Her stomach lurched as she recoiled from him, pulling her hand away from his shoulder.

Open-mouthed, she stared at him.

"You... You shot Joe?"

He showed no remorse as he stood up, his eyes vacant.

"He killed my Cathy."

An uneasy feeling washed over her as her eyes swept around the canal. The barges were quiet with no signs of life and there was no one walking along this stretch of the path, which rarely saw more than a few people a day pass by. Reg was staring at her as she glanced at him. He must have seen the fear in her eyes as he took a step back.

"I'm not here to hurt you."

She felt the comforting warmth of Buster's head nudging her hand and relaxed enough to force a smile.

"I'm glad to hear it. But you realise you have committed a murder."

Reg's jaw tightened as he looked away momentarily.

"He visited us…Joe... at our farmhouse."

His eyes took on a hauntingly dark stare as he looked past her, caught up in the memory.

"He put a gun to my Cath's head. Said he'd pull the trigger if I didn't tell him where Grace was headed. He paused…

"I told him, and he left."

"But the shock of the gun…it was too much for Cath. She had a heart condition, and she died right there in my arms."

His head moved slowly from side to side, his chin visibly trembling as he fought back more tears. Faye's heart dropped into her stomach as she watched him crumble, finally giving in to tears carving their way down the lines on his weary face.

"I'm so sorry Reg. I can't imagine how difficult that was for you."

He lifted his eyes to look at her and nodded, his jaw tensed again.

"It's all in the past now."

He stood up. As he focused on her, his demeanour changed, and he spoke with a clarity that she hadn't heard before.

"That's why I wanted to talk with you at the pub. To explain everything so that Colby could go free. You can tell the inspector it was me who killed Joe."

He stared at her as she wondered why he wasn't handing himself in.

"Yes. Of course. What will you do now?"

His eyes dimmed as if looking into a void.

"I'm going home to say a proper goodbye to Cath."

He screwed his cap up in his hands again, a faint smile spreading across his face.

"Thank you. For your kindness."

Sorrow slackened the lines around his mouth as his jaw drooped. Faye wanted to reach out and wrap her arms around him. His pain was so deep that it reminded her of how she felt when her father, William, died. She still missed him, and no amount of time would eradicate the pain completely.

"And Tell Grace and Colby to take care of each other. My Cath took a real shine to Grace."

Faye could feel tears prick her eyes as he spun around and disappeared back across the fields and out of sight. She whispered,

"I will."

Chapter Nineteen
A Confession

Daniel could see the unease on Faye's face as she walked into the Station House.

"Aunty Faye. You look like you've seen a ghost. Are you okay?"

He stood staring at her as she took off her coat in the hallway. Her mind still turning over her encounter with Reg.

"I'm not sure?"

Her hand shook as she took off Buster's lead and placed it on the side table.

"I've just walked the towpath with Reg... And he confessed to murdering Joe."

Daniel's mouth fell open as he took a sharp breath, and her heart dropped. Everyone was going to have the same reaction, and rightly so, if Reg had murdered Joe. But still, she couldn't shake a feeling of sadness for him, remembering him falling to his knees in grief at the loss of his wife, Cath.

Daniel's voice cut through the silence as he placed his hands on his hips.

"Well, we are a fine pair. I take a kidnapper to a dinner dance, and you take a stroll with a murderer. It must run in the family."

Daniel's humour was lost on her, as she sighed. "That's not helpful, Daniel."

His eyes widened as a thought sprung to mind.

"What on earth is Inspector Rawlings going to say when he finds out you've been cavorting with a murderer?"

A flicker of anxiety crept across her face as she pursed her lips. She didn't like having to explain her actions to Tom. She hung her coat up on the stand.

"It's none of his business who I cavort…walk with." Her chin raised in indignation as Daniel stared at her.

"You are going to tell him?…… Aren't you?"

"Yes. Of course, I am," she snapped. "It would be remiss of me not to. And it would also be classed as withholding evidence."

Daniel nodded his head silently and she could feel his eyes trailing her as she strode off down the hall and past the telephone on the table.

"I will call him when I get a minute."

As the day rolled on, Faye walked to the telephone two or three times, lifted the receiver and put it down again, finding another unnecessary task like dusting the clock on the mantelpiece for the second time and plumping cushions that didn't need any more plumping, until she said out loud,

"This is ridiculous." And marched down the hallway and picked up the telephone receiver. Her heart beating faster at the thought of hearing Tom's reaction to her morning stroll.

The desk sergeant was always happy to speak with Faye, especially as she had brought scones with her on her last visit to the station to make her witness statement about the night Joe was found murdered. After explaining she needed to talk with the inspector, there was a brief pause followed by the sound of the telephone clattering on the desk as he went to inform the inspector. Footsteps returning and the receiver being lifted made her heart beat out of her chest as she heard Tom's surprised voice.

"Miss Lantern. How can I help?"

Guilt caught in her throat as she fumbled her words, her walk with Reg flooding her mind.

"Hello, Tom. I…er… well…I just wondered if you have a few minutes to talk?"

She wrapped the spiral coil of the telephone lead anxiously around her finger, twisting it as she heard the strain in his voice.

"Is it urgent? Only I'm up to my ears in paperwork."

"Well. Yes. I think it is important." She paused, inhaled a deep breath and closed her eyes, rushing her words.

"I had an encounter with Reg earlier today."

She screwed her face up, grimacing as she heard the shock in his voice.

"What... Reg Tanner... The farmer? Faye. Are you hurt?"

He reacted in the same way Daniel had, the same fear in his tone, which made what she was about to say even more difficult.

"No. I'm fine. But I don't think he is dangerous. Far from it. But...he confessed to killing Joe."

She screwed her face up again, waiting for his response, which was not what she was expecting as he said,

"I'm coming over now." And she was left with a clatter of the receiver being replaced and silence.

Faye wrung her hands nervously together, wishing she had told him earlier. A few minutes later, the doorbell buzzed, making her jump. She opened the door, and Tom rushed in, standing in front of her, his eyes darting down the hallway as if checking to see if Reg was still there before looking back to her.

"Faye. Are you sure you are okay?"

"Yes. Quite sure."

She shut the door behind him and walked casually down the hallway.

"I've put the kettle on."

He followed her into the kitchen and put his hat on the table.

"Did Reg come here?"

"No. I met him on the hill by the towpath."

She turned away as his eyes widened in shock.

"The Towpath at the canal. Bloody hell, Faye. Do you realise how remote that path is?"

He had never sworn in her presence before, let alone raised his voice in anger at her. She was about to reply when she felt his hands on her shoulders, turning her to face him.

"I'm sorry, Faye…for getting angry." He shook his head. "I just feel sick at the thought of you being alone with him, with no one around to help."

She felt her heart skip as his eyes met hers, and she wanted to lean in, kiss him, and reassure him she could take care of herself. With such longing between them, it was difficult for her to concentrate as she said,

"I was perfectly safe. I told you. Reg isn't as dangerous as everyone thinks."

Her heart dropped as his hands fell away from her. His face reddened with frustration.

"You just told me he confessed to killing Joe."

He threw his hands up, vexed, as she ignored him and placed the pot of hot tea on the table.

"Yes. But I'm not sure I believe him."

He sighed. "Faye. He confessed. What reason would he have to do that…if he was innocent?"

She pulled her mouth back as Reg's wife, Cath, came to mind. He had every reason to want to kill Joe, but something about him, the kindness in his eyes, just didn't add up.

"I can't say why. I just have a feeling he is lying."

Her hands were shaking, and the teaspoon slid through her fingers, hitting the saucer with a clattering of metal on china. He rushed over and wrapped his arms around her. She fell silent, resting her head on his chest, fighting the sting of tears threatening to roll down her cheeks. She didn't want him to think she couldn't take care of herself and pushed away from him.

With a nod, she forced a smile, "I'm fine."

His questioning eyes still upon her she added, "Really."

He stared at her, and she turned away, busying herself with putting the cups on the saucers. He sat down at the table and glanced over as he drew the plate full of bourbon biscuits towards him, and his tone softened.

"I have two shotgun cartridges found at the scene, which belong to the type of gun used for shooting game." He paused...

"Grace told me she and Colby stopped at Reg's place. That's where I went yesterday. But there was no one there. It was like the house had been abandoned. The front door hadn't been locked, and a shotgun was missing from its place in the open gun cabinet."

Buster sat dribbling, staring at the biscuit in his hand and a smile swept across Tom's mouth. He held up the biscuit, looking at Faye.

"Is it okay?"

"Just one." She said with a fleeting smile, glad Buster had interrupted, giving them a chance to relieve the tension between them. She poured out the tea and sat down next to him as he continued.

"The cartridges found at the scene of the crime are a match for the ones I took from Reg's house."

She sighed, although Tom's evidence was backing up Reg's confession, she still couldn't shake the feeling that he didn't do it.

"I just don't think he has it in him."

He nodded. "You always see the good in people. That's not a bad thing." He raised an eyebrow, inclining his head briefly to the side.

"But even good people can do bad things when pushed."

She sipped her tea, remembering the vacant expression in Reg's eyes.

"He told me Joe held a gun to his wife Cath's head, and the shock of it killed her. She died right there in his arms. He was heartbroken."

Tom's eyes held hers.

"Love will change a man for good or bad, but it will change him. That would have been enough of a motive to push Reg over the edge."

She could feel him continue to stare at her long after his words had faded, and she felt her cheeks burning. Buster whined in the hope of another biscuit being offered and broke Tom's gaze.

"Sorry, Buster. I think that's your lot."

He turned back to Faye.

"Do you know where Reg is now?"

Her mouth curved up into a smile.

"He said he was going to say his last goodbyes to his wife."

The chair grated across the floor as Tom pushed it back abruptly and stood up.

"Right." He leant over, took a few biscuits from the plate, and folded them in his clean handkerchief, which

Faye thought he must carry on him for just that purpose, as he glanced at her.

"Just a few for the road."

She stood up and smiled. "Please. Help yourself."

He tucked the carefully wrapped biscuits into his jacket pocket and looked over to her.

"I need you to go down to the station to make a statement."

Her heart sunk at the thought of condemning Reg, but she knew it had to be done and nodded.

"Are you off to find Reg?"

Tom's back straightened.

"I'm off to arrest a criminal who has just confessed to a murder." He spoke with the authority of an inspector who upheld his position without question. Her head leant to one side, as her mouth pulled back, sadness creeping over her.

"Please give him a chance to explain."

"There will be plenty of time for that when he is behind bars."

Faye turned her head and looked away. Tom had a job to do, but she hoped he would find some compassion for Reg.

He moved closer.

"I have to go."

His face softened as she turned back to look at him.

"I'm sorry, Tom. I just can't help but feel for Reg."

He reached out and pulled her to him again, wrapping his arms around her. She felt the warmth of his body comforting as she rested her head against his as he said softly,

"I promise I will do my best to make it easy for him if he comes quietly."

She sighed. At least she had tried to help Reg.

"Faye, when I get back, I want to talk with you."

Her stomach flipped as she pulled back to look into his eyes. Her heart beat faster as she stared at him.

"I can't explain right now. But I want to try our date again tonight."

His longing gaze at her made her cheeks flush red, and a smile creased the lines around his eyes as she stepped back.

"I'll pick you up at seven o'clock.

He stepped forward again and took her in his arms, his lips touching hers as the sound of Daniel whistling as he came through the front door reached them. He cussed under his breath as he moved away from her and grabbed his hat from the table. With a broad smile reaching across his mouth, he said,

"See you tonight." And took off out the door.

Chapter Twenty
Mrs. Field

Faye could feel her heart racing, thinking about her date with Tom. She had a new lavender blue silk dress, which the store assistant said brought out the colour of her eyes. She turned in the full-length mirror and adjusted the soft scoop of the neck until it was straight. When she opened the door to Tom, his open mouth expression made her feel it was a good choice as he said,

"You look beautiful."

Holding out his arm, they walked down the dimly lit street and into the warmth of the George and Dragon Pub. It was relatively quiet compared with last night's dart team, and Tom didn't have to wade three deep to get served at the bar anymore.

"I'll get mine, Tom." She said, seeing him take out his wallet to pay.

He smiled, passing her a baby sham.

"I would like to buy this for you."

"Thank you, Tom, but you really didn't have to."

He didn't reply as he followed her to a small table nestled by the open fire.

Relaxed, she leaned back in the cushioned chair as Tom took a sip of his ale.

"Did you arrest Reg today?"

He placed his jug of brown ale back down on the table and frowned. He was wearing a cream, chunky knit cable jumper that made his blonde hair and blue eyes stand out. Her stomach fluttered, making her cheeks burn red, and she looked away, embarrassed at staring at him for so long. Luckily, he hadn't noticed as he cast a glance around the bar. A thin, wiry old man in a green woollen cardigan sat in a faded, red chesterfield at the far corner, a pipe clenched between his teeth, reading the paper. Otherwise, they were alone.

He turned back to her.

"Not yet. But my men are on the lookout for him."

She didn't let him see the relief on her face as she sipped her drink, hoping new evidence would emerge to clear Reg's name before Tom caught up with him. But he seemed too preoccupied to notice as he shifted in his seat and gazed back at her.

"I know we haven't been officially dating for long, But I feel like I've known you forever."

She stared at him, her heart racing as he reached for his glass and took another sip of ale, placing it down on the table she saw his hand slightly shaking. He reached inside his pocket and her breath caught in her throat as he knelt down in front of her on one knee. In his hand, an exquisitely cut diamond ring, sparkled against the black velvet lining of the open box.

"I'm in love with you Faye. Will you marry me?"

She raised her hands to her mouth and gasped. Her heart was pounding so hard she thought it would burst out of her chest. Unable to hold back tears, she held his gaze as he stared at her, anxiety and hope filling his eyes.

"I... I don't know what to say?" She had no idea why she said it, as she wanted to say yes with all her heart.

Tom whispered softly, "Say yes."

She could feel her body trembling as she looked at the ring and back to him. Tears rolling down her cheeks.

"Yes."

"It looks like we have arrived just in time."

A shrill voice echoed out as she saw Mrs Field bustling up to them. She glanced at the ring in Tom's outstretched hand as she stood in front of Faye.

"I believe you may want to put that business on hold."

Tom jumped up and went to speak when Faye let out a scream. A tall, rugged man with a shock of auburn hair walked up to them. Mrs Field turned to Tom; her mouth curved up into a smug line on one side.

"Inspector Rawlings." She cast her hand towards the man standing next to her. "Let me introduce you to Tommy, Faye's fiancé."

Love And Murder At The Manor
Chapter Twenty-One
Tommy

The shock on Tom's face shattered her heart into a million pieces as he looked at Tommy standing next to Mrs Field, pain and disappointment filling his eyes as he turned to her. Unable to process it all, she stared, wide eyed at Tommy; he was still as handsome as ever, with dark hair cut short at the sides and green eyes that looked lovingly at her. He rushed forward and hugged her.

"I'm sorry I took so long to find you. But I'm here now."

He stepped back, took hold of her hands, and squeezed them tight.

She could hardly bear to look over at Tom as Mrs Field spoke with an air of triumph about her.

"I believe Inspector, Faye has some long overdue catching up to do, with her intended."

Her words rippled through Faye like an electric shock as she saw the hurt in Tom's eyes again.

"Tom. Please. I can explain."

He had already placed the ring back in his pocket. His eyes flicked over to her hands still in Tommy's. In silence, he turned his back on her and walked out of the George and Dragon. Tears streamed down Faye's cheeks.

"I need to go after him."

"Faye." Tommy's voice calling her name hit her stomach, flooding her with memories as though they had never been apart. She stared at him. Relief, anger and joy rushed through her all at once.

"I thought you had died." She wiped the tears away as more fell down her face.

His thumbs brushed over the top of her hands as she gasped to breathe, and he led her to sit down at the table.

"I was injured and lost my memory. "He shook his head from side to side. "I was in a prisoner of war camp until the end of the war. We were released, and I was sent back home. My father got a specialist to see me, and after two years of therapy, I started seeing your face, Faye. It was as though you were bringing me back through the fog until I could remember who I was again. He dropped onto one knee to face her, exactly where Tom had proposed to her. The old man in the Chesterfield coughed as he looked over at him and back to his paper.

"I've missed you so much. I've dreamt about this moment for so long."

The bar had filled up, and stolen glances and murmurs reverberated around the room.

She jumped up.

"I can't do this here. Not tonight. I'm sorry."

Still on his knee, she rushed past him and fled out into the cold night air. She did not stop running until she found the quiet reprieve of the Station House and closed the door behind her. Her mind ablaze until she wanted to scream.

Chapter Twenty-Two
Reg

The events of last night filled Faye's mind the moment she opened her eyes. Her head still on the pillow where she cried herself to sleep, she stared vacantly at the wall. She pulled her knees up protectively like a barrier to the gut punch she felt, remembering the pain in Tom's eyes before he walked out the George and Dragon. Daniel, calling out as he knocked on the door, brought her focus back into the room.

"Aunty Faye. Are you decent?"

After waiting and hearing no response, he added,

"If you don't answer, I'm coming in."

Faye sighed. "I'm in bed, Daniel. Please leave me alone."

Still staring at the wall, her eye was drawn to the door creeping open and Daniel's head appearing first. Seeing her in bed, he pushed the door open. She could see him staring at her and then walk over with a cup in his hand.

"I've made you a nice cup of Earl Grey."

He hovered for a moment, then placed it down on the bedside table.

"I hear you had a busy evening last night."

His words cut through her, and she turned away, tears rolling down her cheeks. His mouth pulled back as he screwed his face up.

"Aunty Faye, I'm sorry. That was insensitive of me. Is there anything I can do?"

Her mind raced back to the George and Dragon and the pain in Tom's eyes as he saw Tommy.

"No." She mumbled, burying her face into the pillow, her heart sinking.

He stood quietly for a moment. "I'm off to work now, but if you need me for anything, just call me, and I'll come straight back."

She listened to his footsteps treading off the rug and onto the wooden floor as he left the room. In the silence, she could hear the clock ticking, which she had never noticed before. Buster walked in and jumped up on the bed before Faye could stop him. His tail wagged furiously as he licked her face until she had no choice but to sit up, grappling with him, half pushing him away until she gave in and sighed, rubbing his ears until he settled down. As she sat there with Buster resting his head on her leg, she couldn't stop the carousel of thoughts switching between Tom on his knee proposing and Tommy appearing with Mrs Field by his side. Unable to think straight, she sighed again as she scratched Buster under his chin.

"I need a walk to clear my head. What do you think Buster?"

Buster tilted his head to one side as if listening to her. His ear flapping out slightly away from his head. He jumped off the bed and thundered across the room and down the stairs only to reappear in a flash with his lead dangling out of his mouth. She laughed out loud, glad of his company. After a few minutes and with Buster still glued to her side she was ready. She looked down at him.

"Come on then."

A rush of anxiety ran through her body as she opened the front door of the Station House. Peering outside, she said a silent prayer of thanks as she saw the street was empty and quickly made her way towards the canal. Passing the George and Dragon, she closed her eyes. The pain of last night was still crushing in on her. She quickened her pace, and after a few minutes, relief flooded through her as she reached the bench on the towpath. She was greeted by the familiar ducks who came waddling around her feet, looking for crumbs of bread. Buster wagged his tale in greeting, and a smile spread across her face.

"I'm sorry. I haven't got any food for you today."

She sat down and looked blankly at the water ebbing along the canal. A new barge had moored there. Bright yellow and red flowers painted on black wooden panels on the cabin drew her attention. A young boy in a cap came out on deck and waved to her. She held her hand up and waved in a quick acknowledgement of him and looked away. Someone coughed behind her, and Buster's tail flicked from side to side as Reg came to stand in front of her. She jumped at the sight of him, her head full of Tom's warning and what he would say, and she wasn't sure she could handle anymore right now. He lifted his cap to her, a smile edging gently across his mouth.

"May I sit down?"

Her eyes darted around the canal. They were alone and her heart quickened. She wondered where the young boy had gone to. Feeling she had little choice, she gave a half smile and looked back up at him.

"Please do."

He sat down slowly with one hand holding onto the bench, his face contorted for a moment as he lowered his body onto the wooden seat.

"Are you in pain, Reg?"

"Aye, lass."

He didn't explain any further, and she leaned back in silence. Without turning to look at him, she said,

"How did you find me?"

"I knocked on your door. I didn't hear Buster, so I took a chance you might be walking down here."

All Faye heard was, I knocked on your door, shocked that he would risk going to the Station House as Daniel or Tom could have easily answered the door.

He cast a glance around them. "I can see why you would come here. My Cath would have loved it here, too."

Her heart dropped as she remembered his last words to her about his wife Cath and the look of utter despair in his eyes.

"Did you say your goodbyes to Cath?"

His head lowered.

"Aye. I did. Now I have to put things in order."

He turned his cap in his hands, his eyelids heavy as he looked back at her.

"We didn't have children, see. And although we only met Grace and Colby for a bit…my Cath…well…she was taken with them…And her last words were about Grace."

His throat bobbed up and down as he fought back tears. " I followed you here to ask you if you would give this letter to Grace."

He pulled a crumpled brown envelope from his pocket and held it out. She took the envelope and frowned.

"Why can't you give it to Grace, yourself?"

He looked away from her out to the canal. "Because I'm a wanted man. I can't just pop in."

He had a point. She thought. He turned back to her with a smile and that same warmth and kindness in his eyes that she had seen before.

"I wanted to know if young Colby had been released yet?"

Her stomach lurched at the thought of Tom, her words catching in her throat.

"I...I...haven't spoken to Inspector Rawlings about Colby yet. The last I heard, he was still in jail."

Reg's eyebrows furrowed and met in the middle as he frowned.

"I'm going to tell the inspector to let him go."

Faye span in her seat to face him.

"How? You can't go to the police station… not unless you are going to hand yourself in?"

He gazed out across the fields and to the side where the church stood proudly, its spire reaching up, grazing the sky.

"Yes. If I have to, those two young'uns need a fresh start, and I'm not going to be here…."

He clipped his words and fell silent as she stared at him. Jail would probably be where he would spend the rest of his days.

He sighed. "Let's just say I've had my time, and I wouldn't change a thing."

He froze. His eyes fixed past Faye to the Towpath behind them. He looked back at her.

"Please forgive me for this, Faye. But I'm not going to harm you --- no matter what happens next."

Chapter Twenty-Three
A Promise

Fear rooted Faye to the bench seat as Reg jumped up and pulled her up in front of him, using her body as a shield. He pulled a gun from inside his jacket and pointed it at the side of her head. Her body began to shake as he shouted,

"Stay back."

Tom came into view, and her heart jumped. She wanted to say so much to him. Tears cascaded down her face, and Reg gently whispered in her ear.

"It's okay, lass. I'm not going to hurt you."

Tom was standing there with several of his men just behind him, two of them brandishing guns, trained on Reg. Tom glanced at Faye and the gun pointed at her head. He locked eyes with Reg, then putting his arms out, he lowered them, looking back at his men to stand down. Faye was still shaking as Reg spoke to her.

"Promise me you'll give the letter to Grace."

Catching her breath, she gasped. "I promise."

"Thank you, lass." His voice trembled as he said,

"I'm asking you to trust me this one last time, and then you'll be free."

She nodded in silence, and he turned his attention back to the inspector and called out.

"I want to talk with you, Inspector. Just you."

Faye watched Tom say something to his men before walking slowly forward with his hands raised. As he neared them, he cast a glance towards her, his stern expression hiding the panic in his eyes as he looked back to Reg.

"Let's discuss this man-to-man, Reg. There's no need to hold Miss Lantern. You have me now."

After a pause, Reg spoke calmly.

"Inspector. I murdered Joe. This is my confession in front of you and Miss Lantern, who is a witness. You can let that young'un Colby go free now."

Tom stared at Reg, and Faye thought she saw a flicker of compassion fleet across Tom's eyes.

"If you would like to accompany me to the station, we can take down your statement."

Reg slowly shook his head from side to side.

"This is the end of the road for me." He moved the gun away from Faye's head and trained it on the inspector.

"Sit down on the bench, lass."

Faye was shaking so much that her knees gave way, and she fell backwards onto the seat. She pulled Buster closer to her as Reg motioned with his gun to the inspector to move away from the bench. When they were far enough away, Reg glanced over at her. A vague smile clung to his face as he nodded to her. Without a second glance, he shot his gun towards the inspector. Faye screamed.

"Tom."

Another gunshot pierced the air, followed immediately by two more as Tom's men returned fire. She crouched down on the bench and threw her arm around Buster's neck clinging on to him. She heard a thud and opened her eyes to see Reg lying on the ground, and Tom knelt down beside him. He placed two fingers on Reg's neck as Pemberley ran up behind him. Tom turned and shook his head.

"Call the ambulance."

He stood up and wiped a bead of sweat from his brow as he strode towards Faye.

"Faye. Are you injured?"

She shook her head.

"No."

Still trembling, but relieved to see Tom unharmed, all she could think about was last night, and Tommy. "I'm so sorry Tom. I should have gone after you last night when you left." She shook her head from side to side. "I was just so shocked by Tommy that..."

Her stomach churned, plummeting as he cut her words short.

"We can deal with that later. I just want to get you home safely."

He called out to one of the officers.

"Turner. Escort Miss Lantern home."

Her heart dropped as she realised, he wasn't going with her, and she wouldn't have a chance to talk with him. As they reached the bottom of the hill, sirens rang out. Thanking Turner when they reached the station house, she shut the front door behind her, leaned against the wall and burst into tears. Buster, who had walked silently with them, jumped up, and she found herself sliding down the wall on her back, with Buster in her lap, smothering her in wet kisses as he frantically licked her face and hands until she hugged him.

"It's okay, Buster."

She managed to stand up and take his collar off, tears still streaming down her cheeks, as much for her distress over Tom as it was the incident with Reg. A frantic knock on the door made her turn. She opened it and Gwen came rushing in with open arms.

"You poor thing." She hugged her tightly, and with such force, Faye stumbled backwards until Gwen released her grip.

She wiped the tears from her face. "I'm okay Gwen...Really."

Gwen's usual beaming smile disappeared, and her brow furrowed.

"Nonsense. You've had a traumatic experience. It's not every day someone points a gun to your head."

It had actually happened twice in one week, but she wasn't going to remind her as Gwen undid her green headscarf and coat and hung them on the hall stand.

"You need a hot, sweet cup of tea. Come on."

For once, Faye didn't protest about Gwen interfering. She was really quite glad Gwen was there, and within minutes, they were sat at the kitchen table, drinking a hot cup of sweet tea.

Gwen's eyes flicked over to her.

"He's dead, you know...Reg."

Faye stirred her tea, Gwen's voice fading as her mind raced back to the scene of Tom knelt down, checking Reg's pulse. Reg had assured her the whole time he would not hurt her. It was as though he knew what was going to happen. Gwen interrupted her thoughts.

"He shot at Tom, and his men fired back at him."

Faye shuddered, tightening her grip on the handle of the tea cup which didn't go unnoticed on Gwen, as she cast her eyes briefly over at her clenched hand.

"I'm sorry, Faye. I didn't think. You are still in shock." She pushed the back of her blonde, curly hair up and straightened her shoulders. "We have to stay positive and be thankful you and Tom are still here."

Hearing Tom's name jolted an overwhelming sadness in her. Unable to hold her tears back any longer, she sobbed into her hands.

Gwen gasped as she clattered her cup down on the saucer.

"Oh, Faye. I'm so sorry. It's all my fault. I should have just shut up."

She shook her head. "No… it… isn't." she spluttered between sobs.

Gwen jumped up and rushed around the table, putting her arms around her, and leant her head on top of Faye's. She waited until Faye's shoulders had stopped heaving and she was able to breathe calmly again, before she stood back up.

"I'm sorry, Faye. It must have been terrifying for you."

Faye drew in a deep breath and raised her head, straightening her back. Gwen observed her for a moment and, satisfied she was okay, walked back around the table and sat back down.

Faye managed a half smile. "It's not just what happened today with Reg. But…"

Gwen took a sip of her tea, a smile forming on her lips. "Would it have something to do with Tom number two showing up?"

Faye knew how fast gossip spread around the village and lowered her head, nodding slowly.

"Oh, that's not such a big deal." Her smile broadened. "I'd like to have two men falling over me." She pushed a stray curl behind her ear as Faye glanced at her. "It will all work out. Just give it a bit of time."

"You're not angry with me?"

Gwen threw her head back and laughed.

"What on earth for? Tom is my brother, and I love him to bits. But he can take care of himself... and you are my friend..." Her face lit up with that usual beaming smile that Faye had come accustomed to.

"And no matter what happens, you will still be my friend."

Relief flooded through her as a cheeky grin formed across Gwen's mouth. "But...if they duke it out, I'm obviously on my brother's side."

Faye laughed, and Gwen sighed. "That's better. Back to your old self again."

The doorbell buzzed, interrupting them, and Gwen jumped up and went to the front door.

"You'll never guess who it is." She smiled as she walked back in, a glint of mischief in her eye.

"It's your fiancé...Well, one of them anyway."

Faye could hardly breathe as she glanced past her, as Gwen said,

"I'll be on my way then...now you have company," and winked at her. "I'll see myself out.

Love And Murder At The Manor
Chapter Twenty-Four
Tom

Faye stood up to greet Tommy, but he rushed forward and took her in his arms and wrapped them around her.

"I've missed you so much."

She didn't fight him as he held her. A feeling of warmth and security came over her, taking her back to those early days with him.

He bent his head to look at her.

"I came over the moment I heard. Are you okay?"

He spoke so gently that she felt the fear of earlier ebbing away.

"Yes. I'm over the shock now." She rested her head on his chest, and they stayed for a moment, both silent, before she lifted her head up to look at him. Creases around his eyes had aged him, but his look was still full of love for her as he slowly pressed his lips against hers, and she found herself kissing him back. She heard the latch of the front door opening, and Daniel called out.

"Aunty Faye." As he walked down the hall towards them.

She pulled back from Tommy's arms just as Daniel appeared in the doorway. He glanced over at Tommy then back to Faye.

"Ah…It would seem you have a lot of people concerned for your welfare, Aunty Faye."

Tom's tall figure emerged next to Daniel. Hat in one hand, his eyes fell on Tommy. He glanced over at Faye, whose cheeks were flushed with colour.

"I need you to make a statement, Miss Lantern."

His coldness towards her, as if talking to a stranger, made her look away as tears stung her eyes. He was so far removed from Tom, who had proposed to her only the night before. The corner of his mouth twitched slightly, and she didn't know if it was in annoyance or a glimmer of hope that he was as upset as she was. He cleared his throat.

"As soon as possible. I'll be waiting in the car."

Tommy turned back to look at her.

"Would you like me to come with you?"

She shook her head.

"Thank you. But I'll be fine."

He moved towards her. "We haven't had a chance to speak yet…You left so quickly the other night."

Love And Murder At The Manor

Faye felt her stomach turn, remembering Tom's outstretched hand holding the engagement ring.

Tommy gently put a hand on either side of her shoulders. "Faye. Can we start over?"

He looked more handsome than ever as his green eyes smiled back at her, full of warmth.

"It's only fair you give me a chance to explain what happened…why I couldn't get back to you."

She could feel herself being torn, unable to say no to Tommy as part of her needed to know, - yearned to know, why he hadn't contacted her for all those years, but her heart ached for Tom too.

He interrupted her thoughts,

"We could have lunch tomorrow at the pub."

The last place she wanted to be right now was at the pub with tongues wagging after last night's drama, which would now be spreading around the village like wildfire.

She smiled. "Or I could make lunch here for us both."

A broad smile swept across his face. "I would like that."

She stepped back as Daniel, who was still by the door, coughed politely.

"Well. Now that's all settled, I'm off to walk Buster."

They followed Daniel out the door. Tommy stopped and kissed her on the cheek.

"I'll see you tomorrow."

She was acutely aware Tom was waiting in the car with the engine running and her cheeks flushed again as she opened the car door. The short drive to the station seemed to take forever and she couldn't bear the silence anymore.

"Tom, can we please talk."

He didn't take his eyes off the road, and Faye turned to look out of the window as they passed the police station. She turned back to him.

"I thought you wanted me to make a statement?"

His voice was steady and showed the first hint of softness since last night.

"I do. But I want to show you something first. It's not far."

Glad that he was at least speaking with her, she relaxed back in the seat as he swung onto an unmade road. The car jolted as it dipped in a pothole, and she clung to the seat with both hands. He didn't slow down and slammed on the brakes, bringing them to an abrupt halt.

"Here it is."

Puzzled, she looked over at him as he jumped out.

"Tom, what on earth are we doing here?"

He raced around the car and opened the door for her.

"Come on."

In front of her was a beautiful, if not a little derelict-looking white cottage, with a swathe of green ivy clambering across its walls. Tom was already undoing the front door, pushing the pile of letters across the floor as the door opened.

"What's going on, Tom? Who owns this cottage?"

He hurried to the window and pulled back the curtains, throwing open the heavy wooden framed window, letting sunlight flood into the room.

"I do."

He strode back and picked up the pile of letters across the floor and put them on the kitchen table. Faye noticed one letter was addressed to Mr. Frederick Rawlings.

Tom glanced at her as she looked at the envelope.

"This was my father's home."

Sadness crept into his eyes as he looked at the envelope.

"We were happy here…for a short while."

She wanted to reach out and throw her arms around his neck as he looked back up at her.

"Tom"

He held her gaze. "The thing is. I've been in my flat for a while now, and I think it's about time I moved on."

Panic flooded her mind. *What did he mean, move on?* It was the first time he had looked directly at her since he had proposed, and now he was leaving.

"I'm going to do the place up. It's a sturdy building." His head tilted up, and he looked around the room. "It shouldn't take more than a few weeks to get it into shape."

She burst into tears. "You're leaving?"

"Faye." He moved closer to her. "I didn't mean..."

A knock on the door and a high-pitched "cooee." Rang out.

"There you are, Tom."

A slender, elderly woman with whiteish grey hair, neatly swept up into a bun, wearing glasses and an immaculate blue flowery apron over her navy dress, opened the door wide. She was carrying a wicker trug over her arm, overflowing with frothy green foliage, pink roses and twigs with berries. She stood in the doorway, startled as she glanced over at Faye.

"Oh. I'm interrupting."

"No, no," Faye said shaking her head from side to side, quickly wiping the tears from her cheeks.

"Well then, I just wanted to let you know Tom, Cyril will be around Tuesday next week to start on the roof."

Tom, still standing in front of Faye, nodded his head.

"Thank you for letting me know, Lilly."

The silence, still hanging awkwardly in the room, was palpable as Lilly glanced at them both.

"Well, you know where I am, Tom… If you need anything."

She straightened her shoulders and raised her nose in the air. "I'm off to show Margie Field what a tastefully done display of floral art really looks like."

Tom's mouth curved into a smile.

She gave a cursory glance and smiled at Faye.

"Bye, then, my lovelies."

The scent of roses outside the window drifted in on the breeze. A beautiful smell that gave Faye a moment to relax as she closed her eyes and breathed in their sweet, heady perfume. She felt Tom's hand run down her cheek and leant her head into his touch, opening her eyes.

"My father planted that rose as a wedding gift to my mother."

Guilt rushed through her as she remembered Tommy's kiss just minutes ago in her kitchen, and now she was standing here with Tom. She tore her eyes away from his and gazed at the pink tea rose overhanging the window.

"It flowers every year on their anniversary, like clockwork."

He shrugged. "Dad passed away a few years ago, and Mum couldn't seem to find happiness here afterwards. And... well...you know the rest."

"I'm sorry to hear about your father. I know how hard it is to lose someone you love."

She was talking about the loss of her own father, but seeing Tom's expression change as his eyes narrowed, she knew he was thinking about Tommy. He stared at her.

"Do you need time, Faye?"

Her heart lurched. He was prepared to wait for her.

"When you said you were moving on...I realised I didn't want to face each day knowing you weren't there. I love you, Tom."

Shining tears filled across his eyes, and she felt his arms around her. His kiss was so passionate and loving that she felt a lightness as though she could float away on the scent of the roses still filling the room. Tom gently pulled away and reached into his pocket, opening the small velvet box in front of her.

Her breath caught in her throat. "You kept the ring in your pocket?"

His tone now serious.

"You said yes…to marrying me…Do you still feel the same way, now that…?"

He couldn't bring himself to utter Tommy's name, but she understood what he meant.

"Yes. I do."

Her hand trembled as he slid the diamond engagement ring on her finger. His kiss filled with an intensity that made her melt into his arms. Then her mind jumped to tomorrow and her lunch date with Tommy.

Chapter Twenty-Five
Colby

Tom pulled at his collar, loosening the top button of his shirt as sweat beaded on his forehead. He saw Pemberly walking by the open office door and called out.

"Pemberley, can you locate the fan and bring it to the interview room."

The heating had been playing up for weeks, but now it had somehow stuck on full, and they were all sweltering inside.

"Right, you are, sir. And I've called Bob Yates from the village. He'll be over to look at the plumbing this afternoon."

Tom knew how efficient Pemberley was. He was in line for a promotion to sergeant next year until he pulled the trigger on Reg. He would have to go through the standard enquiry procedure, but as a young constable, killing a member of the public who had no criminal record would raise some eyebrows. Tom would argue his case, of course, as he would for Turner, who also fired his gun. He would state in no uncertain terms that Pemberley saved his life, but in his heart, he knew Reg had no intention of shooting him. In the heat of the moment, Reg raised his gun and shot way above his head. It weighed on his mind that it was a deliberate act on Reg's part, knowing he would be shot at close range and likely killed.

"All done," Pemberley called out, breaking his chain of thought.

"Good. Bring Colby to the interview room."

"Right, you are, sir." He rushed off as Tom pushed back his chair and stood up. He shuffled the papers on his desk together before picking them up and placing them under his arm. He walked slowly down the corridor and into the interview room. Colby's eyes darted towards him, full of resentment.

"You can't keep me any longer. I'm innocent."

Tom sat down in silence, calmly thumbing through the papers he had now placed on the desk in front of him. He looked up and met Colby's eyes with a cold, hard stare.

"If you are innocent, can you please explain to me why your fingerprints are all over the barrel of the gun that killed Joe?"

Colby's face drained of colour as he slunk back in his chair.

"I tried to take it from Reg, but he knocked me down."

Tom raised his eyebrows and flipped through the papers on his desk again.

"You said here, in your witness statement, you left Joe alive. Now you're saying you didn't leave, and in fact, you were there with Reg?"

He could see Colby's hands trembling in anger as he said,

"No. That's not what I said. I tried to get the gun off Reg, but he knocked me down." He pointed to the swelling above his eye. That's where he hit me... You saw that for yourself."

An image of a bloodied Colby stumbling out the bushes, blood dripping down from his head as he stood there with Faye, rushed through his mind.

"And that was the last I saw of him, and I needed to make sure Grace was safe."

Tom leaned forward.

"Where did Reg go?"

Colby shrugged. "Into the woods. That's where Joe headed."

Tom ran a hand through his hair as he thought.

"You're talking about the woods on the west side of the Manor House."

Colby shrugged again. "I guess. I don't know."

In a mocking tone, deliberately putting pressure on him, Tom was hoping he would slip up. He locked eyes with him.

"So, you are asking me to believe that you grappled with Reg, and he knocked you down and ran off and shot Joe. And you didn't see or hear anything?"

Pemberley stepped forward as Colby swore under his breath, his temper flaring.

"Y'all aren't getting it. I don't know what the heck Reg was doing there with a gun, and I sure wasn't going to wait any longer to find out. The guy was on a mission and was gone before I got back up off the ground."

Tom sighed, his arms resting on the desk. The cool air of the fan felt good across his face and neck as it creaked around the room and back.

"Did you speak with Reg before he wrestled you to the ground?"

Colby rolled his eyes back. "It all happened so fast. Reg seemed to appear out of nowhere. He raised the gun at Joe, but he dodged to the left, and I ran at Reg. It wasn't more than a few seconds when I hit the dirt, and Reg took off after Joe."

From the marks left in the ground, the flattened grass and broken branches going into the woods, Tom could tell Colby's account had some validity but didn't prove conclusively that he was innocent. He gathered Colby's witness statement off the desk.

"I'm releasing you, but do not leave the village."

Colby's eyes widened, staring at Tom as he gathered up the papers on the desk.

"We've been notified by the state police back home that all charges on you have been dropped. Seems it's your lucky day."

Colby sunk back into his chair. He shuddered. An image of his ex-fiancé vivid in his mind. "About time she saw sense."

Already walking out the door, Tom was oblivious to his comment. Although Reg had confessed to killing Joe, something was amiss; he just couldn't quite put his finger on it yet.

Love And Murder At The Manor
Chapter Twenty-Six
The Letter

The Manor House loomed imposingly over Faye as she stepped up, choosing to ring the bell this time. It clanged out, and she stood waiting for a minute before the door opened.

Edmund's face lit up.

"Faye. How lovely to see you. To what do we owe this unexpected pleasure?"

Her hand rested on the letter in her coat pocket and her mind rushed back to Reg lying on the ground and she half closed her eyes and looked away. Edmund pulled at his Faire aisle jumper, straightening it with a slight nervousness about him. She took in a breath, her mouth pulled back into a tight-lipped smile as she glanced briefly at him,

"I've just come to visit Grace to see how she is." Her smile broadened as she looked up and made full eye contact with him.

"Of course." He bellowed. "Come in. Come in."

Faye detected a note of uneasiness in his voice, he had been affected by this whole business too. An unwelcome scandal that had arrived in the form of Grace followed by two deaths in the village which hung in the air.

"Darling," Elizabeth's voice rang out, her Chanel perfume engulfing Faye as she kissed her on each cheek. Grace was sitting, relaxed on the sofa, smiling as Faye followed Elizabeth into the drawing room. Grace's slim figure looking the picture of elegance in a pure silk, black and white polka dot dress. Her blonde hair tumbling over her shoulders.

"You are looking well, Grace."

Elizabeth leant into Faye and whispered in her ear,

"We are the same dress size." And winked at her.

Faye's eyes widened as Colby walked over.

"Colby!"

His dark eyes danced with happiness. He had an easy way about him, and his American accent felt somehow reassuring as he spoke.

"Faye. I'm sure glad to see you are doing okay."

"Thank you, Colby. I'm glad that we are all here in one piece."

She glanced over to Grace. "I've come to see Grace, actually."

Grace shifted nervously in her seat as Faye pulled the brown envelope from her pocket.

"It's nothing serious…Well, I don't think it is. Reg asked me to give you this letter."

"Now, hang on a minute." Edmund rushed forward. "I believe that it would be in the best interests of Grace if I opened it first."

"Darling, I don't think that will be necessary." Elizabeth whipped the envelope out of Faye's hand and, reading the name, quickly walked over to Grace.

"I believe it is addressed to you, darling."

Grace glanced at Colby, looking for reassurance. He nodded briefly to her, and Faye felt her heartbeat rise in anticipation, staring at Grace as she tore the envelope open. Grace gasped, holding her hand to her mouth. Edmund's face had flushed red as he rushed forward and snatched the letter from her hand. He scanned the page quickly and let out a sigh of relief, handing it back to her.

"Well, that is extraordinary." He turned to Elizabeth. "Reg has left his farm and all his life savings to Grace."

Elizabeth clutched her hands together, a huge smile sweeping across her face. "How positively marvellous, darling."

The chink of the decanter bottle touching the rim of the glass caught Faye's attention as Edmund poured out a healthy-sized whisky and downed it in one. Grace was re-reading the letter as Colby sauntered over to her.

He glanced at the page, his mouth falling open. "Jeeze Grace. You're a pretty rich gal now."

He put his arm around her as she burst into tears. Edmund clattered the glass down on the silver tray and turned to Elizabeth.

"I'm off to see Henderson about taking on some new beaters for this weekend's shooting party." He turned to Faye. "I'll see you out, Faye."

"Oh. Okay then. Well, congratulations, Grace. I couldn't be more pleased for you."

Grace jumped up and rushed over to Faye, throwing her arms around her. "Thank you, Faye, for bringing the letter to me. After what happened to you… well, you didn't have to."

Before she could reply, Edmund piped up,

"Nonsense. All in a day's work. Right Faye?" And ushered her out to the entrance hall.

Feeling like she had been ejected from the house by Edmund as he slammed the heavy wooden door of the Manor House shut behind her, she made her way back along the lane. It was about a thirty-minute walk before the Station House came into view. Her heart leapt in her mouth as she saw Tommy standing under the apple tree, waiting. Casual and handsome in a blue shirt and navy trousers with a cream sports jacket over the top. With a bouquet of flowers clutched in one hand, he smiled with a familiarity that made her feel warm inside as she blushed.

"Oh, Tommy. I'm so sorry."

"I thought you had stood me up," he said, grinning. He held out his arm. "Shall we." Inclining his head towards the pub. "I presume you haven't made lunch."

She felt her heart drop, putting her hand in her pocket to hide her engagement ring.

"Tommy. We need to talk."

Still smiling, he nodded. "Let's go then. I have a lot to tell you."

Mrs Field was walking up the hill on the other side of the road and waved.

"Cooee Faye"

Faye gave a brief wave and put her head down, avoiding talking to her and was thankful to be able to disappear inside the George and Dragon, even though she really didn't want to be there after last night. She took off her coat and sat, hands clasped together as Tommy placed their drinks on the table.

"Were you out walking?" He asked as he sat down.

She shook her head. "Not really. I just had to visit the Manor House."

She tensed up, hardly able to breathe and clutched at her drink, taking a sip to calm her nerves.

"I want to be clear with you, Tommy. So much time has passed. Things have changed…I have changed."

He frowned. "I get that. But I want to give us a chance to get to know each other again."

She shook her head. "It's too late, Tommy. If only you had come back sooner…it may have been different. But …I'm in love with Tom."

He stared back at her. "That can change," he said softly.

"No. It's too late." She held up her engagement ring, her throat constricting as she jumped up from her seat.

"I just can't do this."

She went to walk away, and he caught her hand.

"I'm not giving up on us, Faye."

Tears streamed down her face as she pulled away and ran outside and back to the Station House. She thought it would be easy to just let go. But Tommy managed to make her doubt her feelings within just a few minutes of being with him. She glanced down at the engagement ring on her finger through her tears. This was meant to be the happiest moment of her life…so why was she so upset?

Chapter Twenty-Seven
Evidence

Inspector Rawlings pushed the drawer of his office desk shut. Grabbing his jacket, he flew down the corridor and ran outside and down the steps of Petworth police station just as Mrs Field was turning the corner. About to collide with her, he grabbed the handrail and slowed down enough to stop in front of her. Her thin face was sharp, the contours of her nose like a crow's beak and feeling like she was about to peck out his eyes, he stepped back.

"Inspector Rawlings. In a rush to meet Faye and Tommy down the pub, are you?"

A look of uncertainty crossed his face, and a thinly veiled smile pierced her lips.

"Three's a crowd, though. Don't you think?"

Her mouth drew back into a smug smile as he watched her walk away. His mind raced to Faye and Tommy together. He shook his head and drove the short distance to the Station House. Relief flooded through his body as Faye opened the door.

"Tom."

He noticed her eyes were puffy as though she had been crying. He stepped inside, and she threw her arms around his neck.

"What's this?" he said. His mouth drew into a gentle smile as she buried her head into his chest.

"I just needed to be close to you."

He bent his head down and kissed the top of her head, holding her tight in his arms. He waited a few more moments and then pulled back to look at her.

"Okay. What's going on?"

She looked down sheepishly.

"Nothing."

His body tensed as he stared at her.

"That didn't seem like nothing to me. Faye. What's happened?"

She looked into his eyes. They were so different from Tommy's; they were stern but still full of love. Her head half lowered, remembering the look of heartbreak on his face at the pub; she turned away.

"I went to the pub with Tommy this morning."

His silence hurt her more than any harsh words from him could.

"I told him we are engaged and that I'm in love with you."

She felt his arms wrapped around her again.

"That's good enough for me."

His lips touched hers, kissing her passionately, and she relaxed into his arms. This was where she wanted to be.

Tom sighed and held her close. Buster, barking outside, made Faye jump and drew them apart.

"That's Daniel back from his walk.

She opened the door for them and went to put the kettle on, followed by Tom. As she put the cups out, the telephone rang. She glanced at Tom, wondering whether to ignore it when he reached for the tea caddy.

"I'll make the tea."

She stepped into the hallway; a smile lighting her face and answered the telephone.

"Hello?"

"Faye darling. Elizabeth here. I was wondering whether you would mind asking Daniel if he could pop over and help Grace. She needs an accountant to sort out the money left to her from Reg… Something to do with her being from the States and whether she needs to pay taxes, etc. All boring stuff, of course, but it has to be done."

Faye smiled at Daniel as he came through the front door with Buster.

"One moment, Elizabeth, he has just walked in."

She mouthed to Daniel with one hand covering the mouthpiece of the telephone. "It's Elizabeth. She wants to talk to you about Grace and taxes."

Confused, he stared at Faye, his face screwed up into a questioning frown as she handed him the telephone. Faye made her way back into the kitchen. Buster was sat at Tom's leg, dribbling, waiting for another biscuit.

"That was Elizabeth. She wanted to ask Daniel whether Grace needed to pay taxes back home in America. Tom stared at her with a puzzled look on his face.

"Oh. I forgot to mention that Reg left Grace a letter. He gave it to me just before he..." She didn't finish. "Well, he left all his money and house to Grace."

Tom's expression hardened.

"Faye. That was evidence. And the possible motive for murder. Where is the letter now?"

She felt uncomfortable as Tom stared at her. She should have known that."

"I'm sorry, Tom. I didn't think." She shook her head as she sat down at the table.

"Grace has the letter now...But surely the case is closed. Grace didn't know about the money, and Reg confessed to murdering Joe."

Tom had laid out the tray of biscuits and lifted the teapot, steam rising up from the spout in small spirals into the air as he filled Faye's cup.

"Yes. We were both witnesses to his confession. But something is off. To take all that trouble to make sure we both heard it, so there was no mistake." He shrugged. "It feels contrived to me and doesn't add up. Both Reg and Colby's fingerprints were on the gun. He could just as easily have said Colby killed Joe. We have no conclusive evidence either way."

She thought for a minute as she stirred her tea, the teaspoon clinking as it caught the side of the cup.

"Why don't you go with Daniel to see Grace and get the letter then?"

He nodded.

"I'll have to go now. I can't leave it."

She didn't want him to leave as the image of Tommy filled her mind.

"Now?"

Daniel walked in, overhearing the conversation.

"I'm on my way there now, Inspector. Would you like a lift?"

"Thank you, Daniel. I'll take you up on that offer."

He glanced at Faye, his eye-catching her engagement ring before looking back at her. "I'll see you later."

"Yes. Of course."

She hid her disappointment and smiled as they left for the Manor House.

Love And Murder At The Manor
Chapter Twenty-Eight
Good Fortune

Edmund's eye twitched as Tom walked into the grand entrance hall of Petworth Manor. He thrust out his hand.

"Inspector Rawlings. I wasn't expecting to see you here. And Daniel, my boy. "He proffered his hand to Daniel. "Good to see you."

He turned his attention back to Tom. "What can I do for you today, Inspector?"

Ingrained in him after so many interviews with suspects, Tom studied Edmund's face, gauging his reaction as he spoke.

"It has come to my attention that Grace has some evidence, in the form of a letter, which I need to collect from her as it is now part of an ongoing investigation into the murder of Joesph Maine."

He took his hat off and held it down by his side. A bead of sweat trickled down Edmund's forehead as a smile formed across his mouth.

"Of course, inspector, if it helps the investigation. But surely this is all done and dusted now? I heard through the grapevine Reg confessed."

Tom knew Reg's confession would have fallen foul of the gossip mill in the village and sighed.

"I have to tie up all the loose ends" …he paused. "You understand."

He looked him squarely in the eyes and Edmund coughed, avoiding his gaze and hurried through the hallway.

"Yes. Yes. Come this way."

He opened the drawing room door and saw Elizabeth's elegant frame standing by the long window overlooking the grounds.

"There you are, Elizabeth. Daniel has popped by." He coughed again, with Inspector Rawlings and he needs to see the letter. The one Faye brought over for Grace."

She turned around to face him as Daniel walked in and stood next to Edmund.

"Daniel, darling. How kind of you to come so quickly." She walked over and kissed him on either cheek as Tom strode in behind him.

"Inspector. How wonderful. We were just having some light refreshments. Would you care to join us?"

The one thing the Percys did well was entertaining guests, and Elizabeth's version of light would be far more than tea and biscuits. She pulled the long green chord with a gold tassel that dangled down by the side of the fire place and smiled. Grace sidestepped Edmund and Daniel as she walked in. Her long golden hair now swept up in a bun she moved gracefully in a blue dress dotted with pink blossom. Tom glanced over at her.

"You look very much recovered from your ordeal, Grace. If you don't mind me saying."

A genuine smile lit up her face. "I don't mind at all. I'm feeling much better, thank you."

Colby walked in, glanced furtively at him, and quickened his pace over to Grace. He kissed her on the cheek and walked the farthest away he could be from Tom, positioning himself behind the long table already loaded with tea and assorted bourbons and wafer biscuits. The door opened wide as several maids carrying trays of pork pies, square, pink and white iced cakes and canapes with various salmon, pate and strawberry toppings, trotted over to place them on the table. Elizabeth clasped her hands together.

"Well, this is all rather pleasant. All of us gathered here."

She inclined her head towards Grace and smiled. "Grace darling. Could you please show your letter to the inspector."

Grace glanced at Tom, shaking her head slowly.

"I haven't quite taken it all in. It was such a shock."

She pulled the folded letter from a side pocket in her dress and held it out to Tom. He crossed the floor in a couple of paces and took the letter out of her hand. After reading it, he looked directly at her.

"I will need to take this letter as evidence in an ongoing investigation."

Edmund clattered his whisky glass down on the silver tray and poured out another. Elizabeth's smile faded as she looked at Tom.

"Oh dear. How will Grace be able to claim what Reg has left her? Without the letter?"

Tom pointed to a line on the page. "It says here that he has left an official will and the name of the solicitors."

He turned to Daniel. "I believe Daniel could help you there."

Eager to assist his company's best clients, Daniel rushed forward. "It would be my pleasure."

Tom handed him the letter.

"Good. Take down the details."

Elizabeth flustered around, looking for a pen and paper in her writing bureau as Daniel discussed details with Grace and Colby. Tom turned to speak with Edmund. He scanned the room, an empty whisky glass sitting on the tray, the only clue that he had been there. He walked out of the drawing room as a maid scuttled past him carrying an ornate, silver, metal carpet beater. She disappeared into a side room. The wooden panelled corridor became darker the further he proceeded down it until he reached another arched doorway and entered into the contrast of a bright, airy kitchen. Copper pots and pans festooned on a wooden rack in the middle of the ceiling hung over an enormous wooden table. A plump woman in her early sixties wearing a white apron walked in carrying a brace of pheasants and laid them on the table.

"Inspector Rawlins, what are you doin' stalkin' around my kitchen?"

Tom recognised Mary McBride's stout figure. She had been a cook at the Manor House since he was a young boy.

Re-tying her apron strings, she asked, "How's your mum doin'?"

Her words hit him like a sucker punch to the gut.

She stopped and stared at him, a knowing look crossing her face.

He went to speak, the words not seeming to find their voice; he cleared his throat. "We take each day as it comes."

He glanced around the room. "I'm looking for Edmund."

"Oh. I saw him not five minutes ago, dashing through like a madman, nearly knocked me off my feet, carrying that old bag with rods in."

She turned to the chopping block and placed one of the dead pheasant's necks on it.

His eyes scanned around the room as she pointed, with the large butcher's knife in her hand, to another door leading out of the kitchen. He nodded and set off. A few strides in, he heard the thud of the knife hitting the wooden block as he navigated the twisting concrete steps down into a small boot room. The air was musky, laden with the smell of wet mud clinging to boots lying on the floor. A short row of tweed coats hung on hooks with matching flat caps sat on top. A clatter alerted him to the presence of someone in the next room. He stepped over a stray boot lying on the floor to see Edmund holding up a shotgun, peering through the barrel. The cleaning rod that had clattered to the floor was lying at his feet. Edmund jumped as he saw him walk in.

"You gave me quite a fright there, Inspector. Not many people venture in here."

A glass cabinet door was open, with several shotguns standing against a faded wooden rail inside, holding them in place like a row of soldiers. Edmund placed the freshly cleaned gun back in its holder. Its gleaming barrel is out of place against the dull metal of the other guns. Tom's eye fell on an open box of cartridges inside, and Edmund quickly closed the cabinet door.

"Just a minute." Tom held the door with his hand.

"May I?" He gestured to look at the gun Edmund had just put back.

Taking it from the cabinet, he cocked the gun and looked down the barrel. "Have you done any hunting recently?"

Edmund raised his hand and waved it in the air. "Oh, I don't hunt anymore." He cast his eye down to the open box of cartridges with two missing.

"Occasionally, I take the gun out. But I prefer to host the shooting parties rather than participate."

Tom nodded.

"And when was the last time you fired this gun?"

"Well, now. Emm. Let me see. It was a while ago. I think we were out looking for rabbits. Yes, that's it. I remember now. I went back and got my gun to shoot a few. They have been eating all our crops. Damn, pest they are."

Beads of sweat formed above his brow as he looked back at Tom. His cheeks reddening.

Tom lowered the gun.

"Were you out shooting on the day of Joesph Maine's murder? Last Friday, the twenty-first of this month?"

Edmund's nostrils flared out as he drew in a breath.

"It was a few weeks ago, the last time I shot the gun. And I believe Elizabeth will be looking for us." He opened his hand towards the cabinet, waiting for Tom to place the gun back in its holder.

"Tom continued to hold the gun in his hands.

"This is the same type of shotgun that was used to shoot Joeseph Maine."

Edmund's face drained of colour.

"As you are aware, Inspector, they are very common guns, especially for hunting."

He took the gun from Tom's hands and placed it back in the cabinet. Quickly locking the door with the key, he strode off. Pausing in the open doorway of the boot room, he turned to Tom.

"Let's get some tea, Inspector. I'm sure you're parched by now."

Tom followed slowly behind, his mind churning. Edmund's nervousness was out of character. An uneasy feeling crept over him: Had he been wrong about Joe's death all this time?

Not waiting for Daniel, Tom left the Manor House on foot and reaching the village, he saw Faye standing outside the bakery. He walked up to her, pleased to forget the investigation for a moment and kissed her on the cheek. A smile spread across her face.

"Tom. I'm waiting for Gwen. She asked me for help."

He frowned. "Help? With what?"

Faye's eyes widened as she looked past Tom as Gwen came waltzing down the street, arm in arm with Tommy. Her face beamed as she reached them.

"We've been on a mission." She pulled out some leaflets from her bag. "We have a bit of an assortment to look through."

Faye glanced at the picture of a house and back to Gwen, her mouth falling open."

"Houses?"

"Yes. Tommy is moving into the village. We thought you might like to help him look."

Faye's heart hammered in her chest. Unable to speak, she stared at Tommy. A look of purposiveness in his eyes told her all she needed to know. He wasn't prepared to give her up.

Chapter Twenty-Nine
Colin

The pub was busy as they walked in. Faye managed to find the last table in the corner as Tom bought the drinks over and sat down. He was silent for a moment, and her heart sank as she thought about Tommy. She wanted to reassure him that Tommy moving into the village wouldn't change anything. She glanced over at him.

"You seem preoccupied, Tom?"

He placed his pint of ale back on the table as he looked back at her. "Sorry. It's just this case. I thought Colby killed Joe, and Reg was covering for him." He sighed. "I have a feeling Edmund is somehow involved."

Taken aback, she looked at him. He hadn't mentioned Tommy.

He picked up his glass and took a sip of his ale before continuing.

"I found him acting very strangely. Nervous almost. I followed him into the gun room, and he was cleaning a gun, the exact same type that killed Joe."

Unsure why he hadn't said anything, she decided to forget the whole Tommy thing. If Tom wasn't bothered, then she wasn't going to bring it up. But part of her felt hurt he didn't seem to care either.

"You think Edmund had something to do with it?"

He shrugged. "Now he's found out Grace is his sister; I would say he had a motive, and the scandal it would cause if Joe made any more trouble..."

"What are you going to do?"

"That's the problem. I can't prove anything. Edmund was correct when he said it's a common hunting gun" ... He ran a hand through his hair and leant back.

"I can keep putting pressure on George, but it would be a waste of time with no evidence. He wouldn't admit anything." He sighed. "Or I can file it neatly away."

She watched him wrestle with his mind as he stared into the distance.

"It seems to me that George, Colby or Reg could be equally guilty, and maybe you will never get to the bottom of it, not without any new evidence. And it's a testament to you that you are still trying to find the truth instead of taking the easy route and closing the case."

He looked back at her, his face softening.

"Thank you...For listening and being here with me."

Her heart melted as he stared at her.

"Where else would I be?"

His demeanour changed as he looked past her, and she heard a male voice call out.

"Eh, up."

Colin Stour, Gamekeeper for the Percy's, was standing at the bar, slightly unsteady on his feet. He wore a sage green cap with a peak. A white shirt buttoned up with a black tie, a brown suit, and muddy black boots.

"You off the clock then, Tom?"

Tom inclined his head towards him. "Colin." And glanced at his watch. "No. I'm officially back working now."

He stood up to leave as Colin downed his pint and wiped the back of his mouth with his sleeve.

"You found out who done that yank in yet?"

Irritated, as much for his lack of conclusive evidence as Colin's attitude, he glared at him.

"My investigation is still ongoing." He stood up to leave and kissed Faye on the cheek.

"I'll call by tonight."

Tom walked briskly out the door as she sipped from her nearly empty glass, aware of Colin's eyes boring into her.

"So, you be the lady who moved into the village last year?"

She smiled. "Yes."

"Colin," he said, lifting his cap.

"Faye, pleased to meet you."

"So, you're cosied up with the inspector then?"

Faye felt her cheeks flush.

"I wouldn't go that far. But..." she smiled, holding up her ring finger for him to see.

"We are engaged."

A startled expression fleeted across his drooping eyelids.

"Well, now. That's somethin' I never thought I'd see. Tom Rawlings finally gettin' hitched."

His words were becoming slurred, and she paused, unsure how to respond when he added,

"He's as straight as a dye, that one."

She nodded her head. "Yes, he is a good inspector."

"Colin glanced at her, his eyes holding hers momentarily before blinking slowly.

"Sept' he hasn't got all the facts on this last case with that yank."

Faye finished her drink and walked casually up to him, placing the empty glass on the bar.

"What do you mean?"

"I mean, if he'd have done a bit more digging," he slurred. "He'd have noticed the shell on the far side of the woods."

He nodded, a drunk, slow nod with a self-satisfied look on his face.

Faye frowned. "A shell? "

He called out to the barman."

"Another one if you please, Malcolm."

He looked back at her. "An empty shell from the gun."

"Is it important, this shell?"

"I'd say." His tone mocking. "It's a long way from where the body was found."

Faye couldn't hide the look of surprise on her face. "How do you know that?"

He slowly looked around the bar, lowering his voice to a whisper as he said, "Cause I seen 'em carrying the body."

Faye's mouth dropped open, staring at him as Malcolm the bar tender came over. His white shirt sleeves were rolled up to his elbows showing off thick muscular arms, covered in a large snake tattoo. He placed a pint down on the bar in front of Colin.

"Last orders have been called. That's your last." And walked off before he could argue.

Colin muttered under his breath before turning back to Faye.

"No one knew I was there, see. I was checking the woods to make sure the birds weren't hiding up in the far end away from the beaters; they get a bit clever like that," he added. "And that's when I heard the gunshot and saw his nibs and Reg both standing there. And the yank was lying on the floor…Only it wasn't one of them two, see, that pulled the trigger."

He gave a cautious look around the bar again and began to whisper, beckoning Faye nearer.

"It was one of the shooting parties, only it wasn't no ordinary person; it was one of those titled lot, very high up." He sneered, raising his nose up.

Shocked at what she was hearing, she steadied her voice to hide the panic rising in her as she asked, "Who was it you saw?"

Colin wobbled back unsteadily, his hand just grasping the edge of the bar. He shook his head slowly as he righted himself and glanced at her.

"It's more than my job's worth to say. He shook his head again. "All I'm sayin' is it weren't no murder. It was an accident. The Yank had no business being in the Manor House woods when the shootin' party were out and caught one from one of those top nobbs. She stared, incredulous, at Colin, trying to take it all in.

"So, even though Reg confessed, he didn't kill Joe? …The yank."

"Colin raised his eyebrows and inclined his head towards her. "No. He never killed him…But he did move the body with Edmund."

Faye's heart jumped as an image of Edmund carrying Joe's body came to her. "But why?"

"'Caus no one could be associated with a scandal. They moved him to the far side of the woods to the commoner's ground, where no one was gonna connect it to the Manor House, see."

Faye looked away, her mind racing, "But why did Reg confess?"

Colin looked away from her and took another gulp of his pint. He set the glass back down on the bar, spilling ale over the side. "Caus he was dyin' of cancer. Told me he only had a few weeks to live. And he knew Colby was in the frame for it, ''cause these toffs would have let him hang for it."

She waited for him as he picked up his glass again and downed the rest of the pint.

"Why have you told me this?"

He turned towards her and studied her face, the copious amounts of beer he had drunk making his eyes droop almost closed.

"Caus these sorts always get away with everything. They come down all high and mighty and act above the law and treat us workers like we were the scum of the earth." His demeanour changed, anger flashed in his eyes.

"That toffee-nosed idiot blamed me for not doing my job properly last year 'cause he didn't bag a single bird." He huffed. "He couldn't hit a bird in a cage that one. I just wanted to tell someone, so he didn't get away with it scot-free."

Faye inclined her head,

"But it was an accident."

He nodded.

"As I said, the man couldn't hit the broad side of a barn. But Edmund saw me there just as I was leavin' and called me over. Asked me to keep quiet an not caus a scandal for his nobbs."

That's when Reg told me he was goin' to take the blame."

Faye's mouth pulled back as she thought.

"I need to tell the inspector."

Colin wobbled and grabbed the bar with one hand trying to stay upright. "I'll deny it all, you understand. I can't afford to lose my job."

"I just needed to let someone know the truth. But I'll not say another word."

He placed his finger to his mouth, wobbling and trying to hold it in place, then lifted his cap and staggered out of the pub.

Chapter Thirty
Red Tape

Buster was busy burying his bone under the apple tree of the Station House, pressing down clumps of dirt with his nose over the ground as Tom walked up the path to the door. Greeting Buster, he took some biscuits from his pocket, which he always kept there for him. Buster, joyfully wagging his tail, joined Tom at the door as Faye opened it.

"Tom." She said excitedly as he stepped in. Buster ran past her legs and bounded down the hall.

"I have some news."

Before she could finish her sentence, he reached forward and pulled her into his arms and kissed her. The presence of his body so close to her, sent a tingle through her spine as she relaxed into his arms. He moved back from her, his eyes holding her gaze.

"I'm in love with you, Faye; I should have told you yesterday."

She felt his lips press hers again, gentle but passionate. She knew her heart was his. Breathless, she pulled away.

"Tom. I need to tell you something about Joe's murder."

He moved back, a frown forming across his brow as she said,

"When you left today, I had a conversation with Colin Stour."

Concern filled his eyes.

"He's a drunk Faye. I wouldn't put much store by what he says."

"Well, it just so happens I believe him." She stepped back indignantly.

He put up both hands, sighing. "Okay. Okay. What did he have to say?"

"He said Joe was shot accidentally by one of the shooting party on the Manor House Estate, in the woods by the house."

Surprise crossed his eyes. "The woods by the house? That's not where we found Joe's body."

She shook her head excitedly. "I know. Reg and Edmund moved Joe's body, and then Reg confessed…because he was dying of cancer and only had a few weeks to live. He didn't want Colby taking the blame."

She paused, "because the man who shot Joe is very high up in society and couldn't afford a scandal."

Tom's face was still as he put the pieces together.

"Reg confessed because he thought Colby would get the blame?"

Faye nodded. "Yes."

"And that's why Edmund was acting so suspiciously when I found him in the gunroom."

Tom's eyes hardened.

"I will need Colin to make a statement."

Faye shook her head. "He's afraid he'll lose his job. He said he would deny it if you came after him."

Tom ran both hands through his hair in frustration. She waited for him to stop pacing up and down before she said,

"At least you know the truth now."

He turned to face her. Frustration clinging to the lines around his narrowed eyes.

"But I still have to take Colin in and question him. He is a key witness."

Faye lowered her eyes in thought before looking back at him. "But not if he denies he told me. It will be my word against his. If it was an accident, maybe it's best left as it is?"

She could see him wrestling with the idea when Daniel put his key in the front door.

Faye and Tom stood together as Daniel walked in. He stopped abruptly as he saw them, glancing at Tom, then Faye.

"Well, you're not crying, Auntie Faye. So, all's well."

She stared blankly at him; he seemed unusually tense.

"That's good." He glanced sheepishly at Tom and looked back at her. "Because I have a surprise."

Faye felt her stomach lurch as Tommy stepped up behind him.

"Tommy hasn't got a place to stay, and I said he can take the spare bedroom in my apartment, just until he finds somewhere of his own. I thought you wouldn't mind, being he is an old friend, and it will only be a short while."

Faye drew in a breath, unable to speak, as Tommy walked past her and winked, his green eyes smiling. She noticed Tom's jawline tighten as he gritted his teeth. An awkward silence passed before Tom said.

"I have to go."

He took Faye in his arms and held her tightly. Daniel spun on his heel and trotted off down the hallway. "This way, Tommy."

She felt Tom's arms loosen around her, intensity burning in his eyes as he watched the back of Tommy following behind Daniel.

She lifted her hand and touched his face, bringing his gaze back to her and kissed his mouth. His breath, warm on her neck as he sighed, his arms wrapping around her. He glanced down the hallway and back to her. His chin set firm.

"I'll see you tonight."

Chapter Thirty-One
Edmund

Edmund opened the Manor House door; a look of fear flickered in his eyes as he saw Tom standing there.

"Inspector Rawlings, back so soon?"

Tom's deadpan expression matched the tone of his voice as his eyes fixed on Edmund.

"I need to speak with you regarding your recent shooting party here at the Manor."

Edmund's face turned as white as the shirt he was wearing. He stepped outside, pulling the front door closed behind him. After a nervous glance back, he said,

"Let's take a walk, Inspector." His pace quickened as he headed for the rose garden. Tom noticed the yellow roses and his mind jumped to the night he held Faye at the cottage. He had kissed her with the same sweet smell of a tea-rose that was now flooding his senses. He coughed and cleared his mind as Edmund walked under the green arch of the hedge and into a densely populated arboretum of trees, their leaves gently lifting in the breeze in hues of green, orange and red, encircling them.

Tom looked him squarely in the eye.

"I have a witness who has confessed to being present at the time of Joesph Maine's death."

He noticed Edmund gulp as he continued.

"He has also stated that you were present too, and that it was an accident."

Edmund's face turned scarlet red as he pulled at his collar, loosening his tie, his brow furrowing. He raised his head to a superior stance.

"And what if it was an accident? Not that I am corroborating with this story," He waved his hand dismissing it. "But Isn't it better to let sleeping dogs lie, don't you agree, Inspector?"

Tom felt a spike of irritation run through him. "It is my job to see justice is done and..."

Edmund held up his hand in front of him, stopping him mid-sentence. "But Inspector, surely an accident isn't a crime?"

Tom straightened his back, his tone authoritative.

"That is for the courts to decide."

His cold stare silenced Edmund.

"If the safe handling of a gun hasn't been adhered to, it would then be a case of manslaughter, which is a crime."

Edmund took offence to Tom's statement.

"Now look here, Inspector. I run a tight ship. None of the guns are unsupervised, or, "he stressed. "Unsafe." I stipulate the proper procedures which all the guns follow to the letter. There is no room for error."

Tom took his hat off and held it in his hand. "If that were the case, then Joe would still be alive." He stared at Edmund. "I need to talk with the man who shot Joe."

Edmunds's eyes filled with fear. "All the people who shoot on the estate are highly regarded public figures. Some of the top people in the country," he paused, "including royalty."

His face took on a look of knowing indignation. "I'm sure the police chief may have something to say if you go and stir up unnecessary trouble. And we wouldn't want that now, would we, Inspector?"

His words tore down Tom's defences. He knew it wouldn't go any further than the conversation they were having right now. He sighed. Looking out at the woodland, the light beaming down in the middle of the trees. He looked back at Edmund.

"If this was a murder case, I wouldn't let it stop here.

Relief swept across Edmund's face. "Absolutely, Inspector. I would expect no less." He wiped the sweat from his brow with his shirt sleeve. "Now that we understand each other, I think we can safely forget all this business and put it behind us once and for all. Don't you agree?"

Tom left the Manor House, uncomfortable knowing he would encounter red tape in the form of higher-ranking officers who would tell him to close the case. He consoled himself that it had been an accident, which Colin had no reason to lie about. As he drove back through the village, his mind drifted to Faye and Tommy as he sped up along the road. Tommy would be living under the same roof as Faye. Foolishly, he had underestimated him. But now he saw his intentions; he would do whatever it took to keep Faye. Tommy was not going to steal her away from him, of that he was certain.

BACK PAGE

Discover more from author
Penny Townsend
Visit www.pennytownsend.com for:

New Book Announcements

*

Book Extracts

*

A Q&A with Penny

And sign up to Penny's newsletter to get the latest updates on her books, find out what she's been up to and be the first to know about exclusive offers and news – scan the QR code below:

Printed in Great Britain
by Amazon